THE MAN IN THE LIGHTHOUSE
And Other Short Stories

This book is a work of fiction.

THE MAN IN THE LIGHTHOUSE
And Other Short Stories

Veronica MacDonald

Cover Art by Eliza Tan

Book Layout by Chuck E Johnson

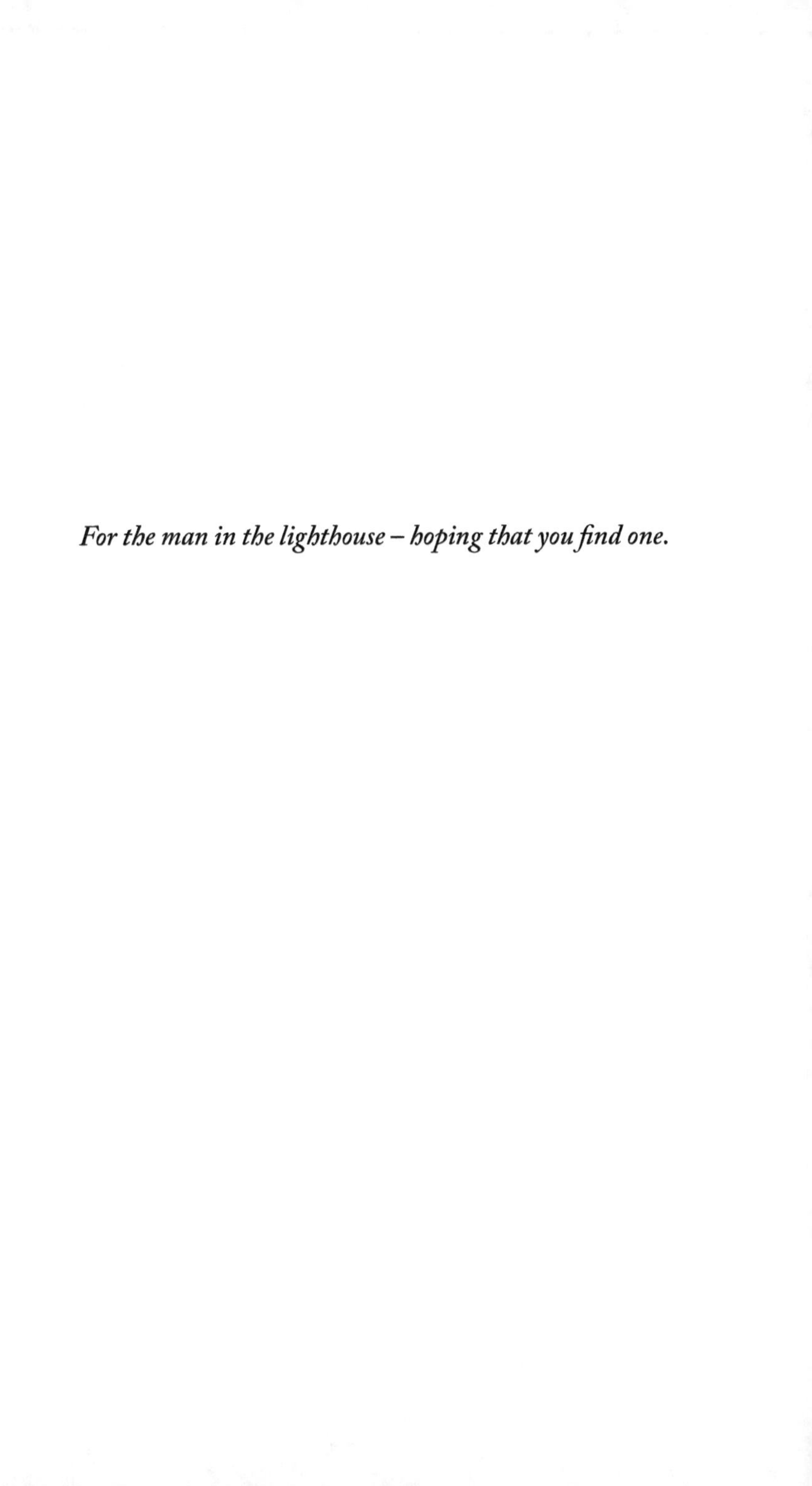

For the man in the lighthouse – hoping that you find one.

We always find something, eh Didi,
to give us the impression we exist.

- Waiting For Godot

CONTENTS

The Man in the Lighthouse   1

The Bride   10

Partial Sky   18

The Graceful Lady   28

All Creatures Unsuspecting   35

Hunger in the Time of COVID   44

Two Shoes   51

The Hat Check Girl   63

The COVID Walk   72

In Honor of Mozart   80

Fairy Tales   94

Green Cars   102

The Wind   114

Beyond Godot   123

The Next Century   136

Night Music   152

THE MAN IN THE LIGHTHOUSE

Birdie walks with hesitancy up the leaf-covered driveway, steps onto the deck, and walks toward the front door of the house. Taking a quick, shallow breath, she rings the doorbell. She stands very still for a long time, but there is no answer.

Little groups of swallows fly overhead, making their way southward to a new destination, and as she looks up to follow their passage, she sees dusty copper wind chimes swaying and tinkling in the breeze, repeating sounds that flapping bird wings might make, flying over.

Thick cobwebs have formed such a solid crown around the top of the chimes that they hold the pipes so stiff that even in the wind they aren't free despite their tinkling. Bending down, she picks up a long piece of pine straw from the floor of the deck and uses it to clean off the mass of web that circles the strings and crevices of the instrument. That done, she tosses the matted pine straw needle over the side of the deck and rings the doorbell once more.

It's early, and the neighborhood, naturally quiet, seems a sanctum of such an abundance of trees, shrubs, and vines that it verges on being overgrown. She sees in the distance a car crawl past the house and disappear around the corner. Anxious that she might appear to neighbors to be out of place standing at a strange door early in the morning, she knocks again softly at the door, yet still hears no sound from within. Her gaze is focused up, surveying pine trees teetering like top-heavy toothpicks, slender and without foliage three-quarters of the way up their trunks. A lemony aroma emanating from magnolia blossoms wafts across the porch. A second glittering chink sounds from the wind chimes, while at that exact moment, the man opens the door.

Birdie glances inside the house before stepping in and notices that he stands barefoot. She looks at him quickly, then back at the chimes, and with an immediate curiosity to know if her cobweb cleaning was sufficient, she grabs the center cord of the chimes and draws the center metal piece against all five pipes. They sing a delicious and full tone as she steps into the foyer of the house, where she stands just clear enough of the door that he may shut it without effort.

Once, Jeff was her friend. Today he will be her lover for the first time, an inevitability neither of them will yet acknowledge. As she stands in the shadow of his aura, she notices a wounded essence buried beneath hauteur, an inclination both frightening yet very, very inviting.

The door now shut to the primitive sounds of chimes and leaves, they stand in the muted den of adobe colored walls and rugs. She looks past the stair railing down into another area of the house, a comfortable room of low sofas and tables, a room she has seen only once, but has returned to see in a new way for the first time.

"Hello, darling, how are you?" Jeff says.

"I'm fine." She clutches her bag closer.

"I was a million miles away," he smiles. "I was dreaming."

Appearing to be a person who would never sleep, one who had no scheduled time nor a need for specifics such as meals common to more plodding individuals, he seems always to be covering two spaces at the same time.

She smiles as she follows him down one flight of stairs. There seem to be staircases everywhere, and one day, not today, she must remember to count them.

"I love this house," she says.

He appears not to hear, as is his custom, to neither register nor comment on a counterpart not his own, but merely poses as a visitor occupying a space in time, like a migratory animal.

"Would you like some coffee?" he asks, which might seem like a natural question because they have shared a cup of coffee many times, but never in his house.

"No, thank you," she says, knowing that coffee alone without the benefit of a muffin or a cookie will only give her the jitters. More jitters she doesn't need. A beer, maybe, but coffee, no. "I'll just have some water," she says. "Water will be fine."

He walks into the kitchen and extracts a hexagon-shaped glass, large and amber-colored like the rest of the house, and fills it with water from the sink.

"What were you dreaming?" she asks.

"I don't remember my dreams much," he says. He takes her hand and leads her from the kitchen down another flight of stairs, across the large sunken room, and into his suite of rooms that adjoin. "I am trying to make an effort to remember them, though," he continues.

"And, how does one do that?" she asks, resting the rim of the glass against her lower lip, sipping as they walk.

"There are ways you can," he says, emphasizing the word 'can.'

Inside the sitting room of his enclosed suite, she feels awkward and on display as never before, and cannot bring herself to look at or touch anything; in fact, she has half a mind to pull out her sunglasses and put them on in an effort to block this nude feeling. Instead, she sits slowly on the love seat across from him and studies an array of pictures on the wall, most of which are newspaper clippings of his various successes. One picture of him, a caricature, smiles at her from the wall. It is a cheerful, younger-looking version of him with an eye-twinkle that the artist has managed to capture; an inkling no longer evident in his face, at least not obvious to the casual eye. She glances at him and sees that he, too, is looking at the picture.

"That is you, isn't it?" she asks.

"Yes, that's me," he says. "Me at an earlier time," he says without regret or apology.

On one side of the suites, a large French Door opens to a deck, and peering out, she can see leaves fall onto the deck. She rises from the love seat, walks to the glass door, and places her face on the cool glass, where in this position, she can see a wooden sculpture hanging high up on the side of the house.

"What a lovely sculpture!" She points up.

He rises from the sofa, walks toward her, and looks out. "What do you think it looks like?" he asks.

She looks again at the piece, "Well, I think it might be just a nice piece of driftwood," she says.

"I know," he says, "but what do you think it looks like?"

"Let me look again." She cranes her neck and presses tighter against the glass, peering at the structure from different angles. Driftwood, like cloud-gazing, can take many forms, and then it can be difficult to explain or interpret to the other person how you formed the image. At home, she owns a piece of driftwood - long like a snake - that had washed up on the Colorado River and was given to her by the only man she had ever loved, a married man comfortable with parting with ambiguous gifts, which could be interpreted any number of ways. "I really don't know," she turns back. "What do you think it looks like?"

He moves slowly toward the door, guru of the manner, smoke rising from his cigarette to cloud the expanse of window, his mind obviously made crystal clear from long days of previous gazing. "A ballerina," he says. "I think it looks like a ballerina."

She moves closer to him and to the glass and looks once more at the greyed wood fastened to the side of the red brick house.

"A ballerina, huh?" She cocks her head to the side, looks up the side of the house, and sees the sky. Though it is only morning, at some point, evening will probably settle upon the room and upon the two of them. "Yeah," she says, "I can see a ballerina. But, I also think it looks like... well, my first impression was of a cow skull."

He frowns through his cigarette smoke and looks long and steady at her, making sense of her answer. His eyes, though puzzled, also sparkle with that same sparkle evident in his picture. Then he looks back outside the window while she continues.

"I say cow skulls because they have a sort of sparse beauty very much like the nature of driftwood itself," she says.

"Hmm," he says, a smile beginning at the edge of his lips.

"Back home," she says, "we used to find cow skulls all the time out in the pasture. Once the bones have been plucked clean by vultures and the bones remain long in the field, the sun bleaches them white, and they look like they have been blown dry by howling prairie winds."

He stubs out the cigarette, a smile remaining slightly on his lips.

"Maybe only I, a born and raised prairie woman, would know that, though," she presses her nose into the glass, and it is cold.

"What, exactly, is a prairie woman?" He laughs a laugh free of malice or mockery that doesn't see silent tears. Most of her tears are silent these days because she has lost the ability to cry.

She walks away from the glass toward the sofa, where he has now taken a seat. As she makes the walk, she catches another glimpse of the picture of him on the wall, still smiling down from his secure stance. On the sofa, she sits on her right foot and leans back into the cushions before she speaks, "A prairie woman is strong. She is, after all, a direct descendant of some of America's strongest survivors. They settled the wild lands in Oklahoma, Texas, and California."

He reaches towards her while she continues, "A prairie woman is privy to dry, barren ground, dust bowl ground which must be coaxed to yield a crop lest she should starve. She lives through things like that. All the women in my family are strong."

He touches her shoulder, "So, what happened to you?" he asks.

She looks straight at him, "I have a great aunt who survived cancer back in the '40s out of spite," she says. "She lived 60 more years from the time she walked away from the doctor's office."

"That isn't as unusual as you might think," he pulls her head onto his shoulder, and they sit for a long, silent moment while outside leaves blow and pound against the glass door like prairie ghosts trying to come in.

He looks back at the sculpture, "I also think," he says in a whisper, "that the driftwood looks like a seagull. Come here," he rises, "I want to show you something."

She stands, he takes her hand and leads her into another room, the bedroom, where he walks to a bookshelf and extracts a book. Lightly, he taps the cover of the book, which has a seagull flying over snow. "I feel a great affinity for things windward," he says.
Now sitting on the bed, he reaches across her and points to a picture hanging squarely over the headboard. It is a picture of a lighthouse sitting off from an ocean background with brick steps leading around the house and up. "That," he says as he points, "is where I would like to live."

"I can certainly see why," she says, "it is beautiful!"

"Yes, it is," he says.

She looks at him in profile, imagining him with cigarette smoke rising, looks at his nice smile that doesn't happen easily, or maybe it happens in a guarded way, like one more accustomed to disappointment than to success.

"Seagulls, lighthouses. You must be a water sign! What is your Zodiac sign anyway?" she asks.

"I'm an Aries!" he says with a frown.

"You're kidding!" she brightens. "You are absolutely my most compatible sign! Not that I actually follow the horoscope or believe in it. It is just very interesting, that's all."

Holding her hand, he reclines, and she lies back onto the pillow with him. Above them, the window is open, and a cool Fall breeze ruffles a persistent cobweb hanging in the outside window glass corner. There is soft music, it moves with the breeze, and she hears for the first time the shard-like sounds of the wind chimes clanging out on the front porch. "Your wind chimes had cobwebs all over them," she says, looking over at him.

"They did?" he has a smile in his voice and in his eyes.

"I cleaned them off with a pine straw needle," her hair spreads over the pillow like molten lava on sand.
"You did?" He bends to place a kiss on her neck.

"Cobwebs interfere with the sharp sounds of wind chimes,"

she says.

"They do?" he lowers his chest over hers and covers her with his body.

"With anything, really. They restrict. They are restrictive, they hold things," she thinks of the freedom with which a spider stalks around the web while its prey lies fully encased.

He buries his face in her hair and breathes, "You smell good," he says.

She slips her hands under his shirt and pulls him closer. Easily, he bares her skin, pulling off garments until she is naked beneath him, queen on a bed of roses.

"I want to give myself to you, but I am too shy to look into your eyes," she says, passion rising in her heart.

"You are so honest," he whispers as he approaches, man in the lighthouse, seagull on the shore.

She of the land, he of the sea, along with stillness, prairie winds, gliding birds, she knows one thing: once this thing catches, it will never let go.

THE BRIDE

Thanks in part to John Steinbeck, Oklahoma suffered for a long time from an inferiority complex. 'Okies,' they called them, rebelled against this stigma and behaved (possibly in an attempt to compensate for their low standing on the status pole) in other dramatic and surprising ways. For instance, Baptist Hospital in Oklahoma City was the first site in the nation to perform sex change operations. Early on, insurance policies issued to government employees carried a cryptic fine-print stipulation: Sex change surgery not covered.

Also, Oklahoma holds the second-highest divorce rate, second only to Las Vegas. Not that this is anything to crow about, it is just a curious reality.

Generalists could theorize (and probably have) that Oklahoma is merely centrally located, and as such, is by default, a type of sociological trend-setting ground. Others have been known to blame the Indigenous people who filtered into Oklahoma, who were driven out of Georgia and the Carolinas in the 1830s during the infamous Trail of Tears. Even non-history students know the "White man" literally stole land from the American Indians. Or, there was another historical fact about Oklahoma that during the 1880s, land was opened up to anyone who wanted to rush in, stake it out, and then rush in and claim it. Therefore, it could be deducted, by some stretch of the imagination, that those same money-grabbing, power-hungry settlers who came flooding into Oklahoma during the land rush were the same archetypal heroes stalking the state many years after Oklahoma land had been "grabbed."

I have my own opinion. Forgetting crooks and thieves and

other name-calling, I submit that only truly strong men and women could have persevered during the land rush in all that dust until dawn and then run in and stake out land, shoving the weak aside. I've even heard stories about how some of them got up in the middle of the night and moved stakes: cheaters they were, too, eh?

Somehow, Jesse James, Pretty Boy Floyd, Belle Starr, and other outlaw friends managed to survive in the caves in eastern Oklahoma, killing their way west, and I suppose the snivelers just packed up and ran off to pan for gold in California.

It is doubtful that any of this is true; it's maybe more likely a coincidence that an overall wackiness generally manifests itself in the inherent makeup of Okies. At any rate, being born and raised in Oklahoma, and proud of it, I was pretty much sheltered from the boredom of normalcy until I moved to Missouri.

The day that a weirdly-dressed, black-haired girl walked into the cosmetic department of Dillard's, the morning had been as fairly ho-hum as usual, with all the fresh midwestern faces standing behind their counters, lined up like obedient little ducklings.

As the girl approached my counter, she lowered her head – an action I interpreted as an apology for her self-imposed, albeit shocking appearance (well, shocking by Missouri standards anyway). She wore all black except for one large, bright red bow, which she had tied, baby-jane-style, around her short, jet-black hair.

"May I help you?" I asked with utmost imagination, brushing aside all those training school spiels about how not to ask

'May I help you' when approaching a customer. Don't ask the customer a yes-or-no question, they said. Yet oddly enough, training often didn't register when a customer was actually standing there.

Startled, she glanced up long enough for me to see beautifully made-up brown eyes. "I was looking for..." she hesitated and raised a long, talon-clawed hand towards the lipstick tester, "a gold lipstick." Her lips and nails, painted a bright cherry-red, matched the hair bow.

"A gold lipstick?" She had caught me off guard. I would have assumed she might have been looking for another shade of red.

She scanned the row of lipsticks at length, then looked at me again. Her face was as white as paste with no blush on her cheeks, and I remembered having read in Vogue that the latest look for Spring this season was going to be what Vogue called 'the whitened-down face wash.' Of course, no one really pays attention to Vogue. Not in Missouri, anyway. Not even in Oklahoma, for that matter. Vogue is, as everyone knows, only for the women in Paris or Italy or far, far away in that global phenomenon known as New York City.

"Yes, gold," she pulled out the center drawer on the tester unit and looked into it. "I am probably going to have to..." Two large hoop earrings, which she wore on the same ear, fell softly forward towards the front of her colorless cheeks as she carefully surveyed eye shadow colors.

"I'm probably going to have to use gold eyeshadow." She looked up again, and this time her eyes wore a new, naked confidence. Yet, it was only for an instant before an accused look darkened her expression, some curse that moves in and lives after years of repeated disapproval in the face of assertion - that curse I recognized well, having achieved it after repeated attempts to foist my own strange ideas onto those who would veto anything original, whether out of habit or out of fear.

"I love your earrings," I smiled.

The girl looked quickly embarrassed at having been found on display. "Thank you," she backed away from the counter after gently shutting the eyeshadow drawer on the makeup tester unit.

She continued backing away, obviously more accustomed to leaving than participating. Maybe she had expected certain reactions, but obviously recognition hadn't been one of them. At least not in middle America, where people relocate to raise children and escape from crime. "Th-thank you for helping me," she said.

"You are very welcome," I said, as I tried to keep my smile sincere.

Like a powdered apparition in a black cloud, she drifted by the other counters, pausing briefly at each one, her presence drawing blatant, open-mouthed stares from the other cosmetic salesgirls. She is just a vision, I thought. A damned hallucination brought on by two o'clock cosmetic boredom. When she walked away, I noticed her shoes were black. They had pointed toes and silver buckles, oddly enough, somewhat like the witch's shoes in Hansel and Gretel.

Such a silence descended over the cosmetic department that one would have thought it was a funeral parlor, a silence that persisted until the girl got out the door and drifted into the mall.

Julie, the salesgirl at the fragrance counter, was the first to speak, "Honey, did you see her makeup? Why, she could pass for the bride of Frankenstein!"

I felt an uneasy dissatisfaction bunching around me like old crows gathering on a stick fence, and I felt strangely obligated to defend the girl.

"I read in Vogue," I said, "that the newest makeup look for Spring is going to be what Vogue called a 'whitened down' look."

"Well, in the first place, girl, it isn't Spring yet," said Julie, "and in the second place, she had no color at all... anywhere!"

"But, that's the look," I continued, wishing I could deliver my defense to an open window and not have to look into eyes.

"No color!" Julie persisted.

"She had color," I said stubbornly, "didn't you see the red bow in her hair?"

A snicker came from one of the girls, a common reaction to my compulsive need to defend underdogs. It had gotten me into more trouble than it was ever worth. Kelly was coming out from behind her counter with arms folded, and was slowly making her way across the floor of the cosmetic department to huddle with all the girls and to engage in gossip. Bored retail employees often succumb to this particular distraction.

Breathing from the diaphragm like they teach you in acting class, I prepared myself to make an announcement. "Being from Oklahoma," I began as sort of a pompous introduction, "I don't think that is any big deal!"

Kelly stopped dead in her tracks and started laughing, "What has Oklahoma got to do with being pale as a ghost?" she roared.

She was probably genuinely curious and dying to know what Oklahoma had to do with anything. I didn't even know myself because when it came right down to it, we weren't talking about makeup at all. We weren't even talking about color or the absence of color, were we? Whatever we were talking about, we were couching it in make-up, yet we had reverted to the age-old arena with the lions and the gladiators and the bulls and the Matadors. The oldest games were still the same games, those between the winners and the losers. Even after having sifted down into the belly of the cosmetic department, we were merely going down for one final win, going for a big fat trophy to display as proof, giving ourselves an exemption ticket like a hall pass, excusing ourselves (the winners) from the responsibility of genuine understanding and tolerance for them (the losers).

"Well," I continued, "being from Missouri, I am not sure you would understand!"

Still laughing, she let out a final puff when she stopped, "That is the most ridiculous thing I have ever heard!"

But I kept going, "It's just that things in Oklahoma are no big deal..." I broke off here, though, because to be honest, this was probably the most ridiculous thing I had said yet.

So, I tried another approach, "People TRY to be different there. They actually pride themselves, if you want to know the truth."

My chest felt hot because I had now started hearing parental tapes about rudeness and this and that, starting to play in my head like a warped sound system. But I was on a roll, and it was too late. I couldn't stop, so I finished up by saying: "I suppose she stands out here in Missouri because everyone here is so ordinary!"

A million pine cone needles could have slithered in the silence. Mouths opened, confusion settled in their eyes, and girls in front of me began to filter toward the safety of their own counters, where they would, no doubt, recover from shock together. I had to acknowledge that my anger was way out of proportion to any perceived assault against society or some poor girl wandering in looking for a gold lipstick.

I looked out into the mall and caught sight of the girl who had now faded to a mere black speck. Her blackness was barely visible as she blended in with the people around her. Together, all the people looked brown and gray, and eventually melted into what looked like a pot of peppered stew.

Behind me, Judy held up a finger, "Look, everyone," she yelled, "I broke a n-a-i-l today."

The room grew hot, and I felt ashamed and embarrassed. Maybe I had been working in retail too long. Maybe it was past my time. I should probably quit. Months ago, maybe. What if I went straight to the Personnel Department and resigned? What would be my reason for resignation? I find it increasingly difficult to tolerate people. Would that be the succinct answer?

Once, years ago, when I quit a perfectly good job, I had actually written that statement on the Resignation Form, but my boss had changed it.

"Type this in that block," he had said, coming back into the room, my resignation wadded up in one hand and a fresh paper in the other. I had read what he had written:

TO PURSUE MORE CHALLENGING AVENUES OF EDUCATION AND EMPLOYMENT.

Maybe I should just take a break. I retrieved my purse, clocked out, and headed outside into the mall, practically floating down the escalator. I felt so light as I made my way toward the exit, passing a hairdo that looked as if it had been blown dry with a vacuum cleaner nozzle while posing, she was, in new white boots, the latest fashion statement for Spring, things being "whitened down" and all. I passed all the white boots that one could buy with just one swipe of a credit card.

I walked outside and crossed the street, headed to Starbucks. I looked for signs of life, for birds, still resting in the south, no doubt. The 'bride of Frankenstein' was nowhere in sight, but I saw a very elderly woman supporting herself with a cane and clutching a brown department store sack that was literally bulging with brightly colored Christmas wrapping paper bought probably half price on a clearance table. That seemed a pretty presumptuous purchase for an elderly woman to be doing at such a time as this.

PARTIAL SKY

Victoria and Jessie walk side by side. Their feet click on the shopping mall tiles, and Jessie clutches her burgundy shopping bag closer to her body. Victoria is small, long-haired, and has a face that is only beginning to graduate from youth. Jessie, the same age, has developed a more contemplative countenance, brought on by the recent divorce.

Victoria looks down as she walks and watches the way her new navy loafers hug her feet. Jessie, sensing an unusual quietness from her close friend, says to her, "You always look down, Victoria. It's like you're afraid of so many things."

"Really?" Victoria's voice sounds far away.

"You're quiet today. All day, quiet. You don't enjoy shopping so much anymore, do you?"

Still, Victoria studies the shoes she bought with but a moment's thought. She was not even looking for shoes that day, but was rather bored and feeling empty until she spied the shoes, picked them up, and turned them in her hand several times. The seams sewn up the back, and the wooden heel is what prompted her to buy them because she had seen very wealthy people wear shoes like this. They would be the perfect shoes to wear with houndstooth, tweed, silk, and Chanel beads.

"Shopping is okay," Victoria shrugs, "It isn't what it used to be. Nothing is, really."

Jessie squints at a large cookie on display in the mall food court vendor case. The cookie smiles with white icing. "It's all because of him," she sighs. "You still have him on your mind. In your every thought. Don't know why you torture yourself like this!"

Victoria's feet feel safe and snug with soft leather wrapped around them like a glove. She just had to wear them the moment she bought them. Just like when she was a child and would buy a new pair of shoes, and her mother would let her wear the new shoes out of the store. Sometimes they wouldn't even bother to carry the old shoes home. 'Just discard them,' her mother would say to the shoe sales clerk.

Already in the new shoes, Victoria has slipped a brand new copper penny through the shoe slots, and looking down, she sees they shine so bright that they could reflect underneath her dress.

"Jessie," she says, "Did you ever hear that Catholic schools wouldn't let girls wear black patent shoes because they might reflect what's beneath their dresses? Have you ever heard that?"

Jessie sighs and switches her heavy purse to the other shoulder, changing hands with the shopping bag. "I think that is probably a gross exaggeration. You hear all kinds of things about the Catholic Church. They've become a running gag for any number of jokes."

She looks at Victoria, who seems to float beside her, hair falling in front of her face as she stares down at her shoes. Two men in business suits pass the girls, and one of them looks at Victoria, momentarily studies her Sphinx face.

"Did you see that, Victoria?" asks Jessie. "See that guy looking at you?"

Jessie turns around and looks at the two men walking in the opposite direction, where she also sees a crowd of other people, and she feels hungry.

"See that?" Jessie persists. "There are lots of guys, guys that look at you, but you never see them. You don't even look at anybody! You don't look at people anymore."

"Really?" Victoria continues to look at her shoes. "Why should I?" She wonders when and if the shoes will begin to hurt as she lifts her gaze momentarily, looking briefly around for phantom men, tosses her hair off her face, yet while looking sees nothing but streams of faceless people, then looks up higher to tiny horizontal windows that line the shopping mall ceiling, "Guess I'm just not interested at the moment."

"I know you're not interested," says Jessie. "That's pretty damn obvious. That's what I'm talking about. You aren't interested. Wish guys stared at me like that!"

"Believe me, it's not that big a deal," Victoria notices that the sun seems to curl into a lazy roll as it shines through the high windows. Beyond what she can see, the sky may be cloudy, but it isn't cold. Clouds like these arrive in early Spring when the days are warming. But beyond a grey sky, the yellow filters through the high horizontal windows, and the mall looks suddenly lit up like a Christmas tree in March. "Jessie, do you notice anything unusual?" she asks.

"I think I notice everything," says Jessie. She looks around her, "What specifically are you referring to?"

Jessie notes that on more than one occasion, Victoria sees things she doesn't see and vice versa: two friends, one with feet on the ground and eyes in the sky, the other with feet in the clouds, and eyes on the ground.

"Don't you feel," says Victoria, "a warmth? I can feel it even though it is happening outside that tiny window," she points. "I always know when Spring is trying to sneak in." She seems proud of her intuition. "I know when Autumn is, too, for that matter."

Jessie repositions her heavy purse again and wishes she could just hand it to Victoria to carry, since Victoria's hands are virtually empty because she is merely wearing the spoils of her shopping day, but she persists in her stoicism and clutches the purse tighter while she looks up at the partial sky peeking through small rectangular windows lining the ceiling of the mall, "Yeah, I see what you're talking about. It's kind of bright."

The girls turn a corner and proceed toward Macy's, which is situated on the far end of the mall. "Victoria," says Jessie, "cheer up! Be glad you are rid of Bruce. You couldn't see what all of us could see. He was downright anti-social."

Victoria stops walking and, with hands on her hips, turns directly toward Jessie as she speaks, "Anti-social? Why would you say that? He was not antisocial! I don't know what you mean by that?"

"Now, don't get upset. Please," Jessie waves at the air between them to wave away any bad energy, gropes for peace, tries to smooth creases that threaten to ripple up. "Victoria, he so much as told you so him- self. Came right out and said it. Those were the very words he used. You told me so yourself!"

"Well, if he did," says Victoria, " it was an honest admission.

Or, an attempt to let me understand him, it certainly wasn't something to use against him." But Victoria lets the objection fade because she knows Jessie is right. He was antisocial. He always questioned things, dissected statements, pounded and pounded, often sifting through conversations until the subject was finished and fully communicated. That was both the reason she loved him and the reason she could no longer tolerate him. His tendency to constantly dig to the bottom of nonsense to merely settle the score had become extremely tiring.

"I'm sorry, Jessie," says Victoria, "you're right. I know you are."

The girls walk through the Macy's lower-level entrance, enter through women's clothes, and begin to trail through various departments. They amble past the luggage department, through men's shirts, and into the children's department. The store is sorely in need of remodeling, and seems to have barely survived the Christmas rush.

Cruising in silence, Victoria spots an unusual visual prop in the children's department: a duck on a pedestal, surrounded by golden leaves and green grass that simulates a pond. The white duck has been expertly stuffed by a capable taxidermist, and as they pass the thing sitting on the pedestal, its blue glass eye gazes dumb and strong. But, upon closer examination, she notices how its white feathers show dirt. It is much dirtier than it would be were it truly alive and able to bathe in the pond. There in the store, however, it is lightly covered with a rust colored dust that settles on deceased things.

"Jessie," I know you won't understand this. You probably won't even agree," says Victoria.

"What's that?" asks Jessie.

"Just let me explain how I'm looking at things," says Victoria.

"You don't have to explain anything to me, Victoria," says Jessie. "I'm just concerned about you, that's all."

"I know you are."

"You haven't been the same since you ran into that jerk!" Jessie stops and leans against a display case that holds folded t-shirts. "Victoria, this purse weighs a ton. Would you mind carrying it for me?" she asks.

"Absolutely," says Victoria, "hand it to me." She slips it over her right shoulder, where it rests beside her tiny black evening-sized handbag.

"Thank you," says Jessie.

"Let me tell you how I look at it," continues Victoria. "I feel him thinking about us. All the time. I know, just know it could have worked."

"Fair enough," says Jessie, listening intently.

"But," continues Victoria, "at what cost! It was just too exhausting. Have you ever tried to thoroughly communicate all the time?"

"I can only imagine," says Jessie.

"I mean, sometimes," says Victoria, "you feel like just once you'd like to go sit in the corner and be quiet, not to have to explain why you're sitting in the corner!"

"I get it," says Jessie. "Listen, let's go back to the food court and get a Coke or something. You hungry? I'm getting hungry."

"Not exactly hungry," says Victoria, "but a Coke, yes."

Re-tracking their steps, they enter the food court and find a table beside a group of teenagers who sit talking and laughing loudly. Strangely enough, a police officer walks by the table and says something to them. One by one, they rise from the table and shuffle away. One of the smaller kids in the group gives the officer an obscene gesture behind his back and they all laugh.

Victoria heaves Jessie's heavy handbag onto a chair right of her, "This thing does weigh a ton. Hope you didn't forget anything!" she teases.

Jessie sets her shopping bag on the other vacant chair, "Watch this stuff. I'll get us a Coke."

Victoria sits and watches the crowd in Jessie's absence. She remembers the dream she had last night. She dreamed she stumbled into Sylvia Plath's house in London years after her death. Everything was still in place, very dusty of course, and she began to snoop around. It occurred to her (in the dream) that she could probably collect some things in a sack and carry them away. But, she decided she had better ask someone first. Suddenly, two people appeared, as people do in dreams, who gave her reluctant permission to extract certain artifacts from the 'shrine.' Suddenly, they began to gather things FOR her - a consecrated effort to keep her from acquiring anything of TOO much value, an odd peculiarity which seemed at this point to be a proverbial parallel in her own life. While she browsed through the London house, two people continued to collect things for her in a brown cardboard box. After they had vanished, as people do in dreams, she began to look through the box. But, much to her disappointment, most of the items were of the scrapbook sort, the kinds of things mothers collect. Those she found of interest, but more interesting were Sylvia's prizes: painted porcelain plates with latticed designs and small hinges. Those, however, would remain behind in the house.

Jessie returns to the table with two tall styrofoam cups. She scoots a cup over to Victoria, plops a napkin down beside it, and hands her a straw.

"Thanks," says Victoria.

"Sure," says Jessie.

"Why do you always end up waiting on me?" asks Victoria.

"You noticed!" laughs Jessie.

Victoria surveys the crowd in the food court. Noisy and messy, the court is dark and depressing with no windows, only fluorescents for light. She wonders if Spring is still banging at the mall's high rectangular windows that show only a partial sky.

"I can't stop thinking about that duck!" says Victoria.

"What duck?" Jessie sucks Coke up to the top of the straw.

"In Macy's. The stuffed duck. In the children's department. Don't you remember it?" Victoria asks.

Jessie shakes her head, "huh uh."

"The one with the dirty white feathers and the blue glass eye," says Victoria.

Jessie leans back in the chair and stretches her legs full length in front of her, "Swear to god," she says. "You don't see two hunks staring you up and down, yet you notice some dead, dirty duck!"

"That is kind of funny," says Victoria.

"No doubt," says Jessie, who is overcome with a temptation to blow bubbles in her Coke.

Victoria begins to twirl her hair between thumb and finger, "I just think it is odd how we preserve things that don't matter anymore." She twirls her hair the way she used to do as a sleepy child, "the duck looked so alive, so much like the real thing. You had to look really close to see that it wasn't alive."

"Yeah?" Jessie abandons any further attempt at understanding her friend. She is tired and wants to go home. Tomorrow is Sunday. Maybe she will go to a movie and sit through it twice. Maybe she will go to two movies. Maybe she will get a part-time job.

"But the living thing has gone someplace else," Victoria continues.

"Uh-huh," says Jessie, crunching ice between her teeth. "Hey, Victoria," she says, "I'm beginning to see how much you and Bruce had in common."

Unhearing, Victoria continues, "The soul, you know. Doesn't it seem odd to you? Futile, I suppose, that this duck might as well not even have been there at all, because it wasn't there at all. Not really."

Jessie savors the carbonation fizz from the Coke in her mouth, "I suppose in some circles it could be regarded as art," she says.

"I suppose you're right," says Victoria.

THE GRACEFUL LADY

I can be shaking the rugs outside and maybe an Elton John tune will pop into my head, and I find myself shaking the rugs to the beat of the tune. After a while, shaking the rug isn't quite as boring since I have a musical accompaniment running in the background. Come to think of it, music must be playing in my head a lot, which I am probably just suddenly consciously aware of at odd times. For instance, while pushing a grocery cart in the grocery store, I might suddenly become tuned into the store's background music and since I know a lot of lyrics to lots of songs, I might catch myself singing along with the music without realizing I am singing until someone stares me down in the spaghetti aisle.

Granted, I enjoyed music a lot, and I must have been a somewhat talented singer, because I auditioned and was chosen to sing in the high-school choir. Also, lyrics, once committed to memory, are able to linger in my head many years after high school graduation, which is how I often find myself idly pushing a shopping cart and singing along.

Honestly, I could raise all kinds of questions about music in schools, such as: why don't schools bother to teach the arts in schools anymore? Why is art of any kind considered non-essential in school? I know all the rationalizations about how 'art doesn't pay the bills.' Well, maybe it doesn't and maybe it does. That debate doesn't come without astute warnings, however, as I remember well Mrs. Davidson warning us in her booming stage voice: only three percent of you will ever become famous, so you should prepare for a career that pays the bills. With that pronouncement, she would often reach in and straighten her bra strap, which, in all four years of high school, I never saw fall once.

Personally, I know someone who actually made it to New York who graduated from our school. He became quite famous and I saw him on television once, but sometime afterward, he was accidentally killed in a car accident in California.

When I would see his name roll on the credits, I recognized it instantly, even though no one but me probably knew that he came from my small town. He stood right behind me in high school chorus and sang in his beautiful tenor voice. If I thought hard enough, I could still visualize him singing the words to one of my favorite songs that we sang in high school chorus:

Give me your tired, your poor,
Your huddled masses yearning to breathe free,
The wretched refuse of your teeming shore.
Send these, the homeless, tempest-tossed to me,
I lift my lamp beside the golden door!

* *

"I hope they don't try'n use taxpayers' money to fix up the Statue of Liberty," the young man who spoke had black hair, wore glasses, and sat on the city bus that swayed slightly with every bump the bus driver hit. He had addressed his comment to an old man who sat beside him, staring straight ahead out the window as if he might be alternately bored, then deaf.

"They say they've completely closed off her hand to whar' you can't even go up in there to look out," he continued his attempt to engage the old man in conversation as we angled up Wornall Street.

The old man straightened sharply, yet continued to gaze directly outside the bus window where he suddenly appeared to spy something of extreme interest, "I seen a lady on a horse killed on that corner," he pointed out the bus window towards an intersection long peppered with fast food restaurants, car washes, and strip malls.

"You take them schools," the young man continued, "just like them schools. I don't think if a person's flunkin' out, he ought to be made to go."

"He hit her," said the old man to the window. "He knowed he hit her, but he jest kept goin' on," the old man slammed a gnarled fist into his open left hand.

The old man noticed that I was watching the two of them, so quickly I ducked my head into the contents of my purse and fished around until I found sunglasses, which I quickly slipped on and promptly averted my head to stare out the opposite window before either of them could catch my eye and begin to talk to me.

The young man impressed me as someone who might be slightly mentally challenged. He carried a threadbare satchel with papers sticking out askew, while using his finger as a bookmark, he held a paperback book entitled Communism and the American Way.

"Thar's jest too many laws already," he continued. "You take them cigarettes. Look what they done to them! 'For long, they're gonna illegalize liquor too, they're gonna put that same warnin' on liquor!"

The word 'liquor' seemed to instantly arouse the old man's attention, and he responded with a jolt, "People just don't care no more!" As he said it, he looked for the first time at the younger man who, though he had been previously vying for the old man's audience, had now focused his attention out the front windshield of the bus as if to aid in monitoring the bus driver's route.

"I don't think nothin' is wrong in moderation," the young man said, removing his glasses and wiping them on his shirt.

"You take them killings," the old man's voice became louder, "people doped up. That's what that is, doped up! They'd kill anybody, they say, just to get that dope!" He began to study the young man with new suspicion.

"And, I don't think they should force all these laws on us," the young man continued to face forward, his glasses now back on his face. "You know, they better be careful," he looked quietly at the old man, "somebody's gonna start a revolution."

When the passenger to the left of me rose to exit the bus, I scooted tight against the window and busied myself watching the passing sidewalk. At first, I began to count sidewalk tiles, but after a while that made me dizzy. It was just another miserable, grey Kansas City day, cold with leftover snow that had refused in two months to fully melt. The snow seemed as oblivious to impending spring weather as the two strangers in front of me were to one another, but in my mind's eye I could still hear words in my head: give me your tired, your poor, your huddled masses yearning to be free…

"Pretty soon we're gonna be jest like Russia," the young man continued. "All them laws. Can't do nothin' unless it's illegal."

The old man raised his hand in a gesturing sweep that spanned the length of the front bus window, "All this used to be land. Miles and miles of pretty green grass," he said. "Sometimes grass," he chuckled, showing a slight softening of expression, "sometimes snow."

"That's why everybody probably smokes dope. That's the real reason, if you wanna know," the young man stuffed his book in his satchel, creating a fat bulge on one side.

"Course, it still could snow," the old man crooked his neck, taking in a solid view of the bus floor while the driver turned a wide corner. "I lived in Kan' City 77 years, and it can snow, now, when it wants to. I'm tellin' you it can!"

The young man stared for a long time at the old man, looked at his rumpled, layered clothing, and looked at the walking stick resting casually between his legs. He brushed dirty, calloused hands through his greasy hair, then ran both hands along his trouser leg as if to wipe away something more persistent than hair pomade. "I don't mind the snow s'much. It's that ice I can't go," he volunteered.

"I seen it come a big one in March," the old man grinned widely at some long-gone remembrance, and revealed toothless gums.

I was nearing my destination, so I pulled the buzzer above the window and gathered my things as I felt the abrupt jerk of the bus coming to a stop. I stepped into the center and walked toward the door, nearly tripping on the walking cane that had begun to stick out into the aisle.

"Sorry, lil' lady," the old man quickly grabbed the cane and rested it safely to the right of him.

"Oh, it's no problem," I tried to smile, and pushed my sunglasses on tighter despite the fact that there was not a single ray of sun in sight.

I was running a little later than usual because I hadn't expected to have to take the bus today. My car had let me down. I badly needed a new car, but cars had risen in price to cost as much as a house once did. Of course, the idea is to keep up with the rising cost of living by making more money, a goal I need to be seriously considering sometime very soon.

Outside, I found the air icy cold, yet I could see brightness on the horizon, and in Kansas City, that is how spring initially makes it's debut: first comes a little light along the mountains, then comes a little flower bud here, a blossom there, and soon we forget those angry days of deep blankets, frozen fountains, and clouded windows wailing in winter nights.

Once outside of the bus, I walked towards the stoplight and got there just as it turned red. Cars from the other direction sped by and splashed spongy, dirty slush up onto the curb. At least the stuff was beginning to show obvious signs of melting. Above the traffic noise, I could hear birds sing, and I looked skyward, but could see no bird-filled trees, only concrete and stone buildings and traffic for miles.

Just as the light turned red to oncoming traffic, one badly-rusted and very dirty car bounded through and turned the corner with a screech. From inside the car, I could hear them shouting in Spanish: Yo tango lechie, yo tango ti..." and then their conversation faded as they sped on. I thought of the boat people in 1978 who were crammed into three decks of a large fishing boat and hoped for a better life as they sailed from Vietnam. I thought of a Cuban war criminal who married an American girl I knew, who had worked hard and became a fairly responsible provider for her. I thought of the Chinese laundry where my one fur coat would be stored come spring. Having made it through one more awful Kansas City winter, I had become obsessed anew with spring, wondering if it would come the same way it did every year: shyly, lazily, and much, much too late.

ALL CREATURES UNSUSPECTING

It is Sunday morning, and she is up earlier than anyone else because she now lives in an old warehouse space downtown where habitation knows no time clock. Except for a remote, passing nostalgia for pastures, ponds, and trees, she loves to fancy herself a city girl.

She ran away from home that summer between high school and college because as much as she feared poverty, she feared the loneliness of the country more - those endless wasted afternoons, that long distance down the dusty lane fifteen miles from town where no traffic ever drove save a visitor once in a blue moon, or gas company trucks who accessed the land through her family's place looking for places to drill for oil or natural gas. Sometimes, cousins would come to visit for the weekend, and she would cry when they left, shedding tears from sheer loneliness.

Holed up in a somewhat sleazy hotel room in the big city with her boyfriend that summer between high school and college, she man- aged to face the gnawing intuition that even her boyfriend might never rise above a certain cultural way of thinking, might never res- cue her from the country, might serve up a life even more bereft than that lonely country existence – a culture not unique to poor, uneducated, southern people. That summer, she went back home and enrolled in college after all, as it was the only escape available. Yet, somehow, education led to a better way of life, and she escaped as soon as possible to the big, cold, hard, exciting city.

The air is cool this Sunday morning simply because it is too early for heat. Early though it is, there is still a steady stream of cars on the road, some with headlights on, some not, so she is careful in crossing at the stoplight, which leads towards the theatre where she and Jake performed last night. Walking beside her on two separate leashes are two dogs: one hers and the other her brother's. He had also moved to the city, had also gotten a good job, and the two were temporarily renting a downtown Warehouse so they wouldn't be immediately dependent on owning cars.

The smallest dog walks very straight and alert, sensitive to every noise around him. He growls low and is ever ready, even eager to bark at anything. The bigger dog, still a puppy, is awkward and bumbling, and he limps and jerks slightly with a nervous twitch, the aftereffects of improperly prescribed tick medication. Her heart often goes out to the big dog or any creatures unsuspecting who, though they are beholden to the hands of caretakers, are powerless to monitor or assure their own adequate protection. "We may have to put him to sleep," the vet had said, "if his trembling gets worse."

The big puppy with its clumsy face looks up at her, and he wags his tail, a too-long appendage which should have been bobbed at birth. He is so large and energetic that when he wags his tail, his hind legs and entire backside sway right along with the tail. His ears flop unevenly over his eyes, and seeing her look at him, he raises his front paws and, with an affectionate lunge, plows against her. "Down, Samson," she scolds.

The dog is bigger than he knows and nearly knocks her down with his weight. He drops down, all fours on the ground, and nudges her leg with his cold nose. She stoops to bend and stroke his head, but the little Poodle runs under her hand and possessively wedges him- self between them.

"You guys be nice," she smiles at their canine innocence. "We are going for a nice little morning outing, and I don't intend to turn back until I am ready."

A few blocks away now, the Sunday morning has become a skyline with building tops shrouded in clouds that end near the upper floors. She looks at the tallest building, the one where Jake said he would never work, and she watches it sleep in its unfinished construction, a crane balanced on top with its tentacle reaching off into the mist. Because of the odd angle at which the crane is balanced, the building looks as if a giant insect is overtaking it like in those movies of the 1950s where a brain was found alive without a body, or an ant might grow large enough to eat Philadelphia. Humanity, relatively protected and innocent back then as to how silent and small real horrors could be, feigned atonement in huge themes not really scary, like blobs overtaking cities or flies crushing buildings as they breezed by.

The dogs, playful and foolish, entwine their leashes with each other and pull her out into the quiet street, creating a long, tangled leash mess in the process. "Guys!" she yells, "Stop!"

The big dog nips with pointed teeth at the little one, who teases him with ornery little pokes in the rear leg with his cold nose. "We are going to go back if you keep this up!" she threatens.

She stops to untwist the leashes, but decides to sit down on the sidewalk while doing it. From her position on the sidewalk, she gazes again upwards at the IBM building, intact except for a few missing windows and absent the little house-like decoration that will soon adorn the top of the building when construction is finished.

Until she met Jake, she had never even come close to knowing anyone solvent enough to work for a company like IBM.

"I worked for IBM as a student intern," he had said, his curly hair forming a soft glow around his face.

"So IBM hires student interns?" she had asked.

"Of course," he had said, "working as an intern is merely a fail-safe program for IBM. If the student doesn't work out, they don't hire them. Then they don't have to bother to fire them." He had spoken this with that specifically sarcastic tone intelligent people often adopt.

"God," she had said, "You must be a brain even to be considered to work there as an intern!"

"No," he had said, "It's just because I graduated from Georgia Tech."

With leashes duly untangled, she decides to cross the street, so she stands and readies herself, but a dirty green car grinds loudly by. Startled, she yanks hard at the dogs' leashes. The three of them stop, and this time she looks both ways before proceeding. Underfoot, red ants trail from beneath a yellow colored vine that grows along the edge of the curb. The ants' string is steady as they proceed and disappear into a hole on the other side of the walk. When she looks up to read the street sign that leads toward the theatre, she decides to go one more block before crossing the street.

"Okay, now run," she calls to the dogs. She holds taut the leashes and the trio quickly dash across the street, as her mission today is to visit in the daylight the place where she and Jake had lain the night before and see if she can find the barrette she had tossed away in frustration.

"Are you engaged?" she had asked.

"No!" His voice had been sharp, off guard. Stern and gruff, he sounded more like the character he had been playing on stage than the person he was: "I'm just not serious."

Silence.

"Are you?" he had asked in disbelief.

There had been a sting to the way he had asked the question, an echo spoken underwater. Above her against the moonlit sky, his outline, cloudy ringlets of hair, eyes green in daylight, had watched her dark in the night.

"Well," she had replied, "I don't touch people I'm not serious about. A touch means a lot to me."

He had not answered. Was he surprised at her implied commitment? That may be the real reason she returns to the scene of the encounter. There may be clues in the grass that last night lay crumpled under their weight.

The dogs stall, pull back, and then turn to eye a movement. The little one barks first, as down the road and toward them a sandy-haired youth runs swiftly, his sneakers lifting him high off the ground. She pauses, both dogs running ahead, and lets their leashes form a 'V.' The big dog begins the tail swishing business again. The boy slackens his pace, his last three steps bringing him to an abrupt stop beside her.

He bends and pets the big dog, "Hello, Samson," he says. He roughs up the dog's ear. "Hey, little Poo," the little dog jumps up on his hind feet, dances toward the boy, and reaches to rest his front paws below his knee.

"Hey, Sis," he tosses a playful Sugar Ray punch at her right shoulder.

Squinting at a sun beginning to rise, he speaks. "Man, you do get up early, don't you?" The sun shines golden highlights throughout his fine blonde hair. "It's Sunday. You should sleep in, Sis!"

"Hey, you should try getting up early sometime," she jockeys, "You might hear the birds sing."

"Well," says Jake, "this guy called." He studies the ant line beneath his sneakers and brushes his toe across the thick stream of marching ants. Seeing him, the big dog licks a big dry gulp at the ants, lifts them with his tongue into the air, then shakes his head.

"Really?" she asks, "What did he say?"

"Nothing. Just called." He bunches his nose up at the sun, "Probably just wants his dog back," he says.

She studies her brother, who is becoming a good-looking kid, not at all the pesky experimental inventor who used to booby trap his room with any number of pranks and pulleys.

"Since I'm here," he says, "I'll walk the dogs back if you want. Think you could spot me the car for just a few?" he asks, an uneven grin on his face.

She reaches up to brush aside bangs falling against her little brother's forehead. There is no sign now on his face of the cheekbone once crushed in touch football.

"Bill, I swear," she begins, "you'd better promise me that you will drive five miles an hour!"

"I will," he says.

"I mean carefully!" she continues, aware that they are no longer driving down long, deserted country lanes, but are driving in the busy big city.

"I will. No sweat," he takes the dogs' leashes in hand and wraps them twice around his wrist. The big dog jumps against him, and the boy braces his stance with slightly parted feet.

"Come on, you imbeciles," he yells affectionately at the dogs. The big one begins to yelp.

"Let's go," the three of them race, with the little dog nearly choking himself because he runs so fast.

She watches Bill fade down the block, then she turns in the opposite direction and presses on toward the grassy field behind the theatre. Her feet padding in soft dirt now, she walks, determined to clear up any misconceptions in the cold light of day without the benefit of softness or breezes or any sweet smells of clover in the night.

The field slants uphill and proves to be nothing more than dried mud bordered by shrub overgrowth more brown than green. On the other side of the mud, the leaves are polka-dotted with holes eaten by insects. Ugly in the light of day - not nearly the vision it had seemed last night. A tractor sits to the side near the edge where mud becomes foliage, and a dirt mattress rests hidden by tall grass. The mud, cracked and dry like the bottom of the Grand Canyon, is surrounded by an arc of bottles and litter. "Why, homeless people sleep here!" she thinks.

She approaches the indention still imprinted in the grass where they had been the night before. "I am not serious," he had said while unbuttoning her blouse. Why would she give herself to those who would abuse and debase her? A girl more in tune with chickens, ponds, smiles, blushes? This was a girl, not city-wise at all. Not really. This was a country girl at heart, hiding in the big city, running away to something unfamiliar and maybe not suitable, a girl bound still, possibly always, to the passivity and the silence of the earth.

She sees her small brown barrette lying on the border where the grass meets the mud. Kneeling to pick it up, she slowly brings it to her lips and feels cool dew that remains from overnight. She feels compelled to work out her uncertainty immediately, yet is unsure what to do. Maybe nothing. It might be refreshing to do absolutely nothing for once.

In every direction, the breeze churns itself, picking up speed on a Sunday morning that is quickly approaching noon. "I am not Prince Charming," he had said.

She steps again onto the dried mud, faces back toward the direction of home, and gropes for her stance in this, another aborted beginning. Too easily the wrenching creeps in and settles like a familiar haze over her patchwork heart. An ant crawls over her shoe and stings the top of her foot. She flicks it away with the tip of the brown barrette. A slight breeze rustles tall reeds, and a tiny brown leaf falls on the tractor seat while somewhere across town, someone else's soulmate sleeps.

HUNGER IN THE TIME OF COVID

When the virus hit, I escaped from the big city to my little cottage by the sea. It seemed like a good idea when this invisible enemy, having swept through Europe into America, left us, one by one, to seclude ourselves while not knowing where to hide, asking ourselves if lockdowns would eventually be enforced by armed men in uniform, as they were being done in Italy.

I could hear military airplanes taking off, flying overhead every 30 minutes. I counted them. They were loud, and there were five, and they were probably flying to assigned virus-imposed duties which we would no doubt be privy to during the evening news. On any other given day, airplanes could be escorting families to vacations, to Disneyland. They wouldn't sound like fighter pilots in training, defending us against an ominous enemy like planes did during World War II, dropping bombs on English citizens who huddled, crowded, but protected, in the underground British railway stations.

I knew a boy born in England during World War II. He told me how he hated the sound of thunder, and his mother said it was probably because he was a baby when German bombs were dropped on English citizens while they crouched and hid. But this lucky girl, born free in America, born to a good family, born after the war, had never until now thought about war, though now facing her own war.

I don't know where I got my big nose because all the women in my family had little ski-jump noses: my mother, Aunt Rea, Aunt Dana, and my grandmother. Even as a child, I wondered about this.

I remember Aunt Dana's ski-jump nose very well, and can

still see her standing over a large blue enamel canner full of newly-sealed, freshly canned tomatoes from the garden, and she would have a little drop of sweat clinging to the tip of her nose, which would never stop her from feverishly trying to finish the canning of summer garden vegetables - not just tomatoes, but squash and pickles and sauerkraut and a goopy conglomeration which I never liked: mixed vegetables.

Having a basement full of canned vegetables was normal for me, as a girl growing up on the farm, and I merely assumed every mother, aunt, and grandmother congregated in the kitchen during summer months, furiously canning to put away for a future time of scarcity like squirrels hiding nuts. Back then, I chalked up this 'food' anomaly to a paranoia unique to those who had endured The Great Depression.

I sit here by the sea, hiding from the virus, stocked up on as much food as I could find in the stores, yet craving vegetables canned fresh from the garden because I am afraid to spend much time in the grocery stores and am accustomed to finding the shelves bare when I do. I'll distract myself by raking leaves from the front yard. Ordinarily, I would pay the yard man to clean the yard, but in confinement such as this, it is a blessing to find a chore that can take place outside, albeit away from people. It's still early, and perhaps I might gather enough courage to venture out to a nearby food store later, which will probably have only frozen food, picked over, never any toilet paper, maybe some yard supplies. I could use a rake to replace this half-broken one that is in dire need of being tossed. Today might be just the day that I feel more brave.

Out of habit, I ignore any people who jog by or ride by on their early morning bike rides or who whizz by on their scooters. I don't intend to be so dismissive; it's just a habit I picked up in busy Atlanta, mingling with those who keep their heads down and press on. But times have changed. Yep, today I might splurge and buy a rake if the store has 10 or fewer people in it, and if no one is coughing, and if everyone is six feet away. I might even linger, browse a bit in the garden department, since gardening is lately my only activity.

With the broken rake, I rake leaves and fallen flowers from the flower bed before I spy a suspicious-looking poison ivy-shaped leaf plant. There are two types of plants with that leaf configuration. One is poison ivy, and one is Virginia creeper. Which is it? There's a jingle, but I can't remember it, but I'm a country girl - I'm supposed to know things like this. I struggle to remember the jingle that I once had memorized. All I can remember is: if it's five, stay alive. Whew! It has five leaves. It's not poison ivy!

I continue to rake, bravely stooping to pick up the spent flowers that touched the five-leaf plant when they fell. No longer worrying about being infected with poison ivy or the virus, I now worry about things slipping away. Those common-sense old-timers, the ones who created the helpful jingles, they are the ones slipping away. If only they wouldn't leave, I would sink my nose into their ancient wisdom like I used to snuggle my little black cat, Simon, before he traveled over the Rainbow Bridge. I still have his little picture on my Facebook page, front and center. He gets top billing, and sometimes I say out loud to him, "Hi, little Buddy. Sure do miss you!" as if he could hear me. Maybe he can. Sometimes, I hope he can hear me, but I'm not going to stop talking to him because if ever there was a best friend, he was mine. I still have his little bed that he only slept in three times. He used to sleep with me until I noticed he could no longer jump on the bed. At first, I'd just spread out my coat beside the bed because he always liked to claim my coat once I took it off. But, I started feeling guilty, feeling that I had ignored him by not noticing sooner that he was getting weaker and weaker and would one day not be able to jump up onto the bed with me. To assuage my guilt, I bought him a snuggly bed to sleep in, but he died three days later. I always seem to wait too long to do the important things. I still have his little bed because I can never find the right time to part with it.

Aunt Dana's pantry would be full of jelly made from the cherries from the tree in her front yard, from pears and peaches from the orchard if the worms didn't get the peaches that year. How I took for granted that extra food, knowing anything I wanted was but a cellar visit away. And, though today, my walk along the beach would grant me all the seashells I could carry home, I could not manifest one fresh vegetable without donning a mask and gloves, going out into the frightening COVID abyss, and hoping the shelves would yield to my hankering.

I'll just go sit in the TV room and watch three little geckos who live outside on the deck. I know they are eating insects. I only hope it isn't termites they are after because today is a day that I am certain the termite inspector is on lockdown. Every day, I have to talk myself down from a ledge of fear and uncertainty. Am I going to run out of milk and peanut butter? Is it just a matter of time before we are forced to choose between standing in line for milk and peanut butter or hunger? I wish someone would tell me.

I've never been hungry until now. Well, I have, but it isn't because I couldn't have anything to eat that I wanted, that there wasn't food nearby. There has always been food in my life. Like an insensitive voyeur, I've been vaguely aware of news stories featuring the hungry, the "food-deprived," they call them. I have half-heartedly watched broadcasts of children whose main meals were eaten at school, have seen compassionate food banks serving lines of the hungry homeless, and have heard countless family stories of hunger, which, up to this point in life, I've never felt.

Twenty years after her death, I still own a pair of Aunt Dana's house slippers. I go and put them on, hoping to draw her closer in the effort. The slippers were new when I acquired them, as she had duplicates of everything, especially house slippers, which she became fond of after she installed that brand-new gold, sculpted carpet over her hardwood floors back in 1963. She said the hardwood floors were too much trouble, didn't leave her enough time to cook the chocolate pies, the lemon pies, the peanut butter cookies, and her daily freshly baked bread. People dropped by her house often and would usually say, "Just stopped by to see you, didn't come to eat." But she would cut the pies anyway, and they would eat them anyway.

I loved Aunt Dana's staircase because it curved and turned a corner. Although she didn't actually need those two extra bedrooms upstairs, as she had no children except me, and I was just on loan while mother worked, she definitely did need those extra closets be- cause they were full of family photos, obituaries of people she had known, of hand-made doilies she had crocheted, of dolls she had made, of first-class blue ribbons won at the state fair for perfectly canned pickles, okra, green beans and asparagus spears standing up straight in jars like good little soldiers.

She did die one day, unexpectedly, after having outlived her husband by nearly 18 years. But she had lived the American dream, and independent to the end, she died in her own two-story house. Also, I believe she died a painless death because she died of a stroke that took her so instantly that doctors assured the family she probably never even suffered pain, and in fact probably didn't even know it had happened. By sheer coincidence, I had spoken with her two days before to let her know that I had booked my bi-annual trip home and would see her soon. Her last words to me were, "I can hardly wait." Years later, I drove by her old house when I was back home and noticed that the place looked deserted and the door was standing open, so I pulled into the driveway and parked. Inside the house, there were leaks in the ceiling, and her sheer curtains still hung above the windows. One of the window panes was broken out, and a puff of breeze blew the panel into the room where it danced like a lonely ghost. The mirror over the fireplace was cracked, and if I ever had any suspicion that one day Aunt Dana might haunt her beloved house, I now knew better. She would have never allowed it to look like this.

My mother died during the time of COVID, but not from the virus. She died with a hopeful heart, as she was looking forward to my visit in the spring, "if we can get rid of this COVID thing," she had said. But one night as she slept, she passed on without me.

Today, I am so hungry I am tempted to go back to Atlanta, to join my husband, who is brave enough to stare down this virus head-on. I am tempted to make reservations at Petite Auberge - force them to open up and serve us. We would sit in one of those booths with individual lamps at each booth, my husband and I. Pulling off one of my black evening gloves, I would grasp the slender stem of my glass of Pinot Noir and ask, "So tell me, darling, what did you do today?"

But, wait. If this is just a movie that I'm living through, it isn't a big-budget film with crystal chandeliers and staircases that wind and turn a corner, and with jazz music in the background. This is a horror film. Ok, so be it! Horror films can be quite glamorous. Perhaps at the table in Petite Auberge, after pulling off my black evening glove, I grasp the slender stem of the glass holding my Pinot Noir, not realizing that perhaps the waiter has dropped a bit of poison into my glass, and I sit there wondering if this sip shall be my last.

Suddenly, I'm out of the mood to go to the store, to any store. My garden gloves only have one hole in them, and the rake, though half cracked down the middle, can still rake leaves. I still have dried spaghetti on the shelf and a can of tomato sauce, and some leftover beer bread. I feel like the girl in an old black and white film, who had been holed up in her apartment, hiding from the Police. In the movie, when the police had finally tracked her down and banged on her door, she opened it, knowing full well that she was about to face the consequences. She looked at the cops, and holding up a cigarette, she said, "I have only one cigarette left. Should I smoke it?"

TWO SHOES

"You must be the woman I've been waitin' on all morning!" She was sitting at a table with a sign overhead that said: DO NOT SIT AT THIS TABLE. FOR APPLICANTS ONLY.

Above her head, cardboard ceiling tiles were stained brown and hung buckled and torn. Rusted pipe and metal gridworks from the floor above showed through the ceiling tile hole.

The girl at the table heaved her large bulk out of the chair, clutched her Dukes of Hazzard lunch pail, and pulled her coat tightly around her as she waddled toward me.

She followed me as I walked to the window, where a yellowish man in front of me smiled behind greasy glasses and began to type something on an old standard typewriter. He ripped it out and shoved it toward me.

"You are to report to this address," he pointed to the address on the form with his pen, "And you will receive a dollar for every person who rides with you." He glanced and nodded slightly at the large girl standing behind me.

She extended her hand towards me, "Hi, my name's Helen, but you can call me Angel."

Nodding to her, I looked back at the address on the form and realized that it was in a small neighboring town that I had no idea how to find.

"Is she to ride with me?" I asked the man at the window.

Angel grinned at me, showing badly rotted front teeth with

swollen, reddish gums above them.

"Yes, if you don't mind," he said. "You see," again he pointed to the form with his pen, "You get a dollar for every person who…"

"Good, I'm glad because I have no idea how to get there," I said.

"Oh, I can show you," Angel appeared anxious to be helpful as she wrapped a dirty red scarf around her neck and pulled matching red gloves from her coat pocket.

We drove to the warehouse, and she showed me where to park, pointing with her finger and saying it was "where we parked before."

When we arrived at the warehouse, I opened the car door and looked down into a puddle of squishy mud, as it had been raining all morning. Sidestepping the mud the best I could, I climbed outside into the dampness and headed, purse under arm, towards the large building before us.

Angel knew which door to enter, and once inside the warehouse, she immediately spotted the person to whom we were to report, a wispy-haired woman in a purple sweatsuit. She leaned closer to me, "You're gonna love this place. We get two 30-minute breaks and one 30-minute lunch." With that, she promptly plucked the work form from my hand and, presenting both of our forms to the girl, announced, "We are here from the personnel pool."

The woman held a burning cigarette in one hand and several work forms in the other. She took a slow drag on the cigarette and looked suspiciously at my skirt, then down to my shoes, then up once again into my eyes. She blew out the smoke, walked ahead of us, and waved us forward with the forms, "Follow me."

We walked past tall steel corridor racks stacked high with various boxes and pieces of plastic-wrapped equipment. As we went deeper into the warehouse, the temperature dropped sharply, and I was beginning to wish I had kept my coat. A dim light shone before us, and as we neared it I saw a grubby little corner squared off, cleared away like a rat's nest. Peeled label backs and squashed boxes lay in piles on the floor. The woman handed me a stack of labels, wrapped in a rubber band. With the cigarette still posed between 44two fingers, she pointed toward a stack of boxes, "These get one stack of labels." She traced a 45-degree angle in the air and pointed again, "Those get two, and up to eight over there." She pointed high and to the right.

I looked at Angel, who nodded, "Just like we did yesterday."

Not pausing to acknowledge, the woman continued, "You can stack the finished boxes there," and she pointed to a short wooden pallet sitting nearby. She looked at me once, then at Angel, whose head was still bobbing up and down in agreement. The woman threw her cigarette stub on the floor, squashed it with her foot, then turned and walked away.

Angel knew how to fold the boxes and what forms to insert, and even how many boxes to stack on the pallet. She talked almost non-stop with a chatter that I tried without success to tune out.

"You'll have to excuse me if I talk like a trucker 'cause I am a trucker," she said.

"You are?"

"Yeah, I'm just doin' this while I'm waitin'. I'm just dyin' to get back on the road." Her nails were short, bitten down into the quicks, and her fingers were red and swollen as if she worked with cardboard boxes by day and bit her nails by night. In the little squares of nail left, she had residues of purple nail polish.

"Oh, so this is just temporary work for you, too?" I asked.

"Yeah," she said.

"While you are waiting," I said.

"Yeah," she talked without looking up.

"Are truck driving jobs hard to find?" I asked, more out of challenge than curiosity. Obviously, this girl, if she were old enough to drive a truck, had been banned for some highway violation.

"Not if yor good. I had everyone tell me, Angel, they says, well... Angie... they call me Apple Angie. That's my handle. They says, Angie, you got three strikes against ya. Yor a woman, yor five feet four, and you was born with polio."

I took a better look at her standing there, "But, you aren't crippled," I said. "Thank goodness."

"Well, you see these shoes?" She pointed to white vinyl tennis shoes, "They have an arch in 'em this high," she traced an arch alongside the side of the shoe. As she bent down to do this, I noticed the woman in the purple sweatsuit watching us from a glass window far away.

"An' I says… you watch me!" She continued talking, oblivious to the inhospitable surroundings.

"When do you expect to go back on the road?" I felt guilty egging her on, yet I continued anyway.

"Well, I gotta go ta court first," she said. "For rammin' a guy."

"Ramming a guy?"

"What was I s'pose to do? This guy stops alongside the road, and he had a gun, so I just mowed 'em down," she said.

In the dark distance of the warehouse I heard a sound like a low whistle, then heard someone shouting, "BREAK TIME!"

Swiftly, Angel dropped the labels she had been holding. "This is a good place ta work," she said.

She waddled towards her purse, and as she bent to retrieve that and her metal lunch pail, her ponytail, held neatly with a rubber band, flopped to one side and her blouse rode up over pink bulging flesh to show tops of purple terry undies.

In the break room, six people sat at a long table playing cards. The head mogul appeared to be a skinny guy in dirty navy-blue work clothes who spoke nothing but profanities.

"Bid, slut!" he held a wooden match in the left side of his mouth, and it bounced when he spoke as if it were permanently hinged. "Damn it, sumbitch, wha'd ya do that for?"

To the right of me a nervous-looking young man sat wearing a black billed cap, yellow plaid shirt and brown corduroy pants. He was thumbing through the newspaper, "A 14-year-old girl was raped again on Independence Avenue." His skin looked pale beneath the black cap.

"Yeah, bastard, what the hell were you last night?" The skinny man tossed a card into the center pile and rubbed his beard stubble with the back of his hand.

"That makes two this week," the young man turned a page.

Angel sat to the left of me. She opened her lunch pail, then closed it again. In the presence of strangers she seemed suddenly shy, not at all the songbird from a few minutes ago, and I wondered if the men made her feel uneasy. She picked up her purse and began to lay objects onto the table. "That's what I'm lookin' for!" She produced a large bag of salted nuts. "I just love these. Buttered peanuts."

I picked up a thick paperback that had emerged from her purse and opened the cover.

"That's real good," she smiled, "I'm about halfway through it."

I read the inscription just inside the cover, a dedication to someone other than her, a dedication as if this were a treasured, classical novel.

"Eight-year-old kid kills an 80-year-old woman," the young man rattled the paper as he read.

"Yeah, bastard, what the hell were you?" the man at the table laughed a raspy laugh.

The pale boy looked over at the skinny card player, "with that 14-year-old." A loud chord of hoarse laughter rose from the men at the table and filled the already smoke-filled room.

A timid lady across the table whispered quietly to the skinny man, who now had a huge stack of cards raked in and lying in a pile in front of him, "Did ya see her car?"

An embarrassed silence fell over the group, and the loud man spoke up, "Nope."

She glared at him, "You said you did!"

"Seen her car!" he reared back. "When!"

Her face, though pretty, was showing harshness for her young age. "What kind of car is it that I want real bad!?" she exclaimed.

He looked at me, pointing the matchstick right at my nose, "A Chrysler LeBaron convertible?"

I looked into his yellowed eyes, eyes gone too long without proper nutrition, eyes too deep into smoke fumes and alcohol to turn back. I felt naked in a room of encrusted coffee cups, filthy ashtrays, faces and mouths. "Yes.." I said.

"My god, I couldn't even afford one a' them sons-a-bitches when I was makin' $20,000 a year! What the hell do you work?" he demanded.

Angel stopped chewing and looked at me, her Barbie Doll

thermos posed in midair.

"What the crap 'r you doin' here?" He made an attempt at a sensual smile, one mouth corner turned up, the other anchored to the matchstick.

Angel began to fold up the top of the peanut package and stuff it back into her purse. A black girl down at the end of the table turned her cards face down on the table, "Damn it, Carl, if you don't shut up 'n pay attention, I'm gonna' cut off your hello and stick it in yor right pocket!"

The whistle sounded out in the warehouse. Angel rose from the chair and gathered up her lunch pail and bulging purse. "Break time's over," she shoved the book at me, "You can read it at lunch if you want."

We walked back into the chilly darkness and took our position in the filthy corner. A radio blared an old Rick Nelson song, but I felt so removed at the moment from any sibilance of culture. His music seemed utterly lost on us, coming from one who, during his lifetime, lived in luxurious seclusion somewhere in Beverly Hills. Split from this sphere completely, the gap seemed about as accessible as the planet Mars, and as familiar as the bottom of the deep blue sea.

After only four hours, the boxes began to cut into my fingers, and the palms of my hands felt as if they might be forming calluses. More to the void than to Angel, I spoke, "I cannot believe what I have done with my life."

I could smell body odor similar to salted potato chips, one that often lingers on clothes washed out in the sink, "All for the sake of an acting career. See, I'm an actress," I said to

Angel.

"Yeah?" she grinned at me, her two front teeth showing a blackened rot.

I felt foolish talking in elusives to one barely in touch with survival, yet I continued, "Well, I have never actually gotten paid - all just community theatre. But it has kept me from committing to anything meaningful. I mean, I have always been struggling at acting, and sometimes I..."

She seemed genuinely interested as she continued with automatic hands to fold and tape boxes.

"Sometimes, especially lately, I think I am never going to make it," I said.

"Well, my Daddy used to say: 'Angel, they can't never take away yor dreams. They can take away yor cigarettes, they can make you quit yor drinkin', they can far you from yor job, but they can't never take away yor dreams." Her face shone with a distant light like the sun illuminating a skyline beyond hills of snow.

"Your Dad sounds like an intelligent and sensitive man," I felt small tears right behind my eyes.

"Yeah, he's a trucker and he's own the road," she looked above me as she talked. "But, you see, I had a dream of becomin' a country 'n western singer, and I can sing just like Patsy Cline, note for note." She moved her head to the side, her ponytail punctuating each word, "So, one night I had a dream that me and Patsy Cline was own the stage." She looked at me as she bent to pick up a folded box, "Together, we was own the stage of the Grand Ole' Opry, and I tole it to this woman and she says it was an omen."

"An omen?" I said.

"Yeah, she tole me it was," said Angel.

"Do you mean like a lucky omen?" I asked.

Again, she looked at a point above my head, storyteller fabricating her tale. I scanned her young face, clean except for remains of purple eyeshadow creased in her lids.

"An omen! Yeah, an omen!" Her voice ticked up with a tinge of exasperation, as if she didn't really know the definition of the word 'omen,' that it was just a word that she was repeating.

"You see, I'm just waitin' for the other shoe to fall," she continued, her hands spread apart as she had quit folding boxes for a moment. "One shoe done fell when I had this dream. In life thar's two shoes," she bent to pick up a flat box, then straightened again, "And, I'm just waitin' for the other shoe to fall."

The Beatles now sang on the radio. From the naked bulb above us, a halo of light cast a circle, leaving the rest of the warehouse in a darkness broken up here and there by small shadows. The poker-playing crew, buried deep in the bowels of the place, was strangely quiet, alive only a few minutes each day.

"One day on the road I found this lil' dog in a box," Angel continued, "this box was just sittin' out in the middle of the road. I geared that sucker down eight times and ran back and got the box out of the middle lane."

The peeping window behind us sat unmanned and silent, looking into the dark like a gaping hole. "Angel," I said, "Once, Jack Nicholson said... do you know who Jack Nicholson is?" I asked.

She stood looking sideways, her mouth half open in a puzzled smile.

"He said when he accepted his Academy Award... he said something like this: 'you...' he meant us, people like you and me, he said to everybody watching: 'you deserve the award. You are living life. We are only playing it.'" I had said this to my silent partner standing beside me, her eyes crinkled at the corners in little tucks as she continued to listen to me in dull amazement.

"For a long time, that made me feel better," I continued, "kind of took away the guilt I feel at never having achieved any measure of artistic success. Like, maybe it's okay to not be famous. Maybe it's really more important to endure life day by day, uneventful as that may seem." I was spilling thoughts out into the void, and I knew it.
Her hands worked more slowly now. Her smile, reaching for understanding, seemed permanently affixed, a Mona Lisa fortress guarding a wealth of innocence. Two bright cherry-colored food stains rose and fell with the efforts of her breathing.

I stood solidly now in that other plane like in a time warp, seeing more clearly into the banquet where the rich, if they are beautiful, are the rulers, where the illusion is the reality, where the warrior, if he dies, becomes the hero, but where the ugly, the mundane and the fallen are the forgotten.

Deep into the warehouse, the radio blared loudly into the silence…
"Oh, yeah, life goes on
Long after the thrill of livin' is gone"

THE HAT CHECK GIRL

"Three to two," Jerry waves a fist in the air at the opposing baseball team. He looks with an old concern at his silent wife, but he only looks for a second. Ball fever runs deep in his blood and soon he rants back toward the field, shouting loudly: "ONE OUT!"

A blue-hatted man holding a child by the hand passes by his seat and Jerry takes this opportunity to yell at him. At games Jerry shouts at anyone who will listen, "There will be 30,000 people in this stadium when he plays here again!" he yells to no one in particular.

The casual passerby ignores Jerry much like his wife does, and maybe for the same reasons, but this doesn't register, and he waves back toward the field shouting into the wind, "The man's dust! DUST!"

A black man walks by the seats wearing a concession badge, a picture identification of himself on his apron. He carries a red crate full of beverages as he shouts above the crowd, even above Jerry, "Coke here! Ice cold Coke here!"

This triggers something instinctual in Jerry and without hesitation, he stands and motions toward his wife's knee for her to move aside. He leaves his seat, moves first into the aisle, and then makes his way down into the concession stand. Stella now alone, feels vulnerable, and turns her body mostly away from the handsome young man who is sitting the second seat down. When the home team scores against the opposing team, she claps, opens a bag of peanuts and turns to the young man with the bag stretched forth. He shakes his head no into the wind, and she extracts two fat peanuts still in their shell, and presses them into his hand.

Jerry returns to his seat holding a beer in each hand. The wind blows and catches her hair as she looks up at him, tiny gold hoop earrings blowing lightly against her face.

"Didn't I tell you?" Jerry yells in unison with the crowd, his voice drowned in a wave of shouts and claps. Far in the distance, the concessions man stands and pours beer from his case, his level gaze an unseeing attempt to make enough tips to keep the rent going. Pouring until the foam rises an inch over the top, he wipes his hand on a towel attached to his apron, buries the suds-covered bottle in his crate, and lifts it up again.

When the young man vacates his seat, Stella assumes her former low-energy profile, scoots lower in her seat, and focuses solemnly on the field.

"You're getting a suntan," Jerry looks at her face, looks for some clue, some quick-fix for a 10-year malaise.

"Uh hum," she shakes her head at the field.

"There he goes! Hits another one! B-o-o-o!" Jerry rises from his seat with the crowd. Stella stands too, mostly because everyone else does, and the package of peanuts peeks out from her right rear jeans pocket. The organ plays a song, the crowd quietens, and they all sit back down.

The handsome young stranger returns and passes in front of her seat. She squints up at him into the sun and makes an exaggerated scoot backwards as if to make plenty of room for him to pass. The stadium speakers loudly blast Oklahoma Border Line.

Stella asks the young man a question in the noise, "Haven't I seen you down at Tony's?"

He looks at her, not sure that she has spoken to him, "Beg your pardon?"

"I work sometimes," she says, leaning toward him from her seat, "as a hat check girl at Tony's."

"Oh, Tony's. Yeah, I go there sometimes," he says. "I'll probably be there New Year's Eve."

Stella smiles, the stranger settles in his seat, and she points like a child into the sky, "Look up there." The red-white-blue flag stands straight out in the wind, "Sure is windy."

Jerry slaps her shoulder heavily, a big rough paw upon a once delicate arm now grown slack through disappointment. She and her husband rise, leave the game and go home where she sleeps like a woman drugged. The phone wakes her like a fire alarm screaming through the night.

"Hello," she feels a hangover-type headache.

"Stella, where are you? You're supposed to be here by 7:00. Are you working tonight? Maybe I'm confused." Once again, Goldie has had to call to remind her to come to work.

"Sorry, I didn't forget. It's just that Jerry and I went to the game and I took a nap afterward. Must have overslept. I'm pretty exhausted, but I'll be there."

In the club she smells the familiar aroma of baked potatoes and fried shrimp. At least this is a step up from the Green

Frog Cafe. Tony's is next door to Cowboys, a country western bar, and the music is so loud that it blares through the walls as if they were made of rice paper. From the Cowboy bar, sappy singers reminisce of Kansas City Nights, Broken Hearts, and Steady Rain.

"Hi, hon," Goldie meets her near the front door as if she has been waiting for her for a week. "Hurry, slip in there," she points to the hat check cubicle by the door, "Tony hasn't even missed you yet."

"That's good. Thanks, Goldie, I really appreciate it," Stella says.

Goldie purses her lips and shushes her, "No time for that." She then hoists her round cocktail tray above her head and throws a glance over her shoulder as if to scout for one more thirsty customer or an empty glass. "Just promise you will mention to your doctor that those pills are making you too drowsy." Goldie looks back to the silence, "Will you?"

Stella nods, thinks of the handsome young guy at the game and feels hopeful, "Yeah, promise."

Goldie saunters into the recesses of the restaurant, her long hair kissing her waist. The phone rings intermittently in the cubicle, but even that will become routine after a while when customers get their reservations solidified for the evening. Then the backup line can be used behind Tony's back for sneaked calls between staff and sweethearts. She sees it happening all the time.

The air is colder with customers going out than coming in because the OUT door aligns perfectly with the hat check booth. Once the air suction is even strong enough to blow to the floor a grey tweed hat, which she moves quickly to replace, before its owner discovers its shoddy treatment and fails to tip.

Faintly in the background a man's laugh drifts forth, and although she should be wondering what Jerry found to eat, she is really wondering if the young guy might come in tonight. On some level it registers that she is merely entertaining a foolish dream, but she cannot afford to face that fact. Not right now, anyway.

A couple on their way out stroll by, hand-in-hand, cowboys sing of long blonde hair and Ruby, just as another customer releases a cold breath, and another, and then two more.

When she first started this job she used to say goodnight to everyone who left, but by now that has gotten really old. Now she reads magazines and self-help books designed to tell people in 300 pages or less how to take charge of their lives, how to transcend their addictions, and how to rediscover the zest in their marriages. Jerry says he doesn't understand why she doesn't just read fiction, "At least you can learn something of value that way," he once said "especially if you read one of those historical novels."

As the evening progresses, the Cowboy Club acquires a live disc-jockey who is now winding up for free dance lessons. She can hear the announcement on their speaker system through the thin walls. She sits, stares onto the cold street, wonders if she will still be alive come New Year's Eve.

A male customer breezes through the door, walks up to the counter and leans on it, "Hi Sweetie."

With each customer it is different. Should she be cool? Should she be friendly and smile ear to ear? Maybe she should drape her hair over one eye, lean forward and croon, "Hi-i-i-i."

She wants a glass of wine, but no one has come to check on her for a while and she certainly dares not leave the station. Instead, she makes a sort of psychological study of people who frequent the hat check booth. The friendly diners who walk out sweetly saluting "goodnight" are the older, more settled people. These are the people who are said to have 'built this country' whatever that means, or they are also referred to as the salt-of-the-earth. These are the people who think 'goodnight' means 'goodnight' in any tone of voice and usually don't analyze such nuances as tone of voice, tilt of head, or expression of face. Oddly, she often feels more alone as a victim of obtuseness than anything, a subject no self-help book has yet touched upon.

"Goodnight," she says smiling thinly.

"Goodnight," the man returns, he, well-fed, probably heading for home and the fireplace.

Rock and Roll sneaks into the cowboy tunes next door and lends an unsettling aura. Oddly, she finds country music one of the few things left that is basic and secure in a fast-changing world.

Goldie comes to the rescue with a glass of wine at about the same time a blue jean-clad girl staggers into the hat check cubicle looking for a pay phone. "Goldie, I have to be honest. This isn't as much fun as it used to be," Stella leans her chin on her propped-up hand. "Honey, you name me one thing that is," she twirls on her spike heel, hair flying behind her in a circle, which when teamed with circular cocktail tray, resembles two perfect commas.

"But, it is only nine o'clock," Stella calls after her as if Goldie were the Fairy Godmother who could make it all go away. She adjusts the portable heater to blow directly at her feet now, and in bending down, sees fresh car headlights pull in. At nine o'clock a new crowd will be arriving, a younger, more daring crowd. They normally run around without coats and she welcomes the slack in business. Plus, they frequently come in the wrong doors. The cowboys are two-stepping now, and she has the urge to quit her job and go next door and apply for a new job. She also wants a cigarette, but she quit smoking two years ago and most of the time doesn't think about it.

In the background, the cash register chugs along promising that at least the club is making money, for it is difficult for mechanical devices to fake things like being busy or not being busy. Outside in the streets a siren sounds, she needs the ladies' room, but it is way down the hall. Not that she is guarding any high-dollar minks or anything, but sure as shootin' if she were to leave the station for even something necessary, the owner of the grey tweed hat might pick that very moment to forfeit his claim ticket.

The cashier comes to chat. She is an attractive, well-preserved senior citizen with bleached blonde hair and immaculately painted fingernails coated with Revlon Pink Pearl nail polish. She lives in an apartment and doesn't seem to worry about the fact that at her age she still has acquired no real estate.

"Boring night?" she asks.

"Pretty much," Stella answers, resisting the temptation to make up juicy stories and lies about tips. "Makes me think maybe I should have gone into beauty college right out of high school instead of hanging out, thinking I had some gift to give the world."

Betty strokes her bouffant blonde hairdo with the palm of her hand, "Child, everyone has some gift to give the world."

"You think so?" Stella hesitates to draw her out on the subject even though she desperately wants to latch onto an uplifting comment or two.

"Yep, baby, we're all here for a reason," Betty smooths her tight pants over that skinny butt that old women get while their stomachs bloat and make up for any falsely perceived thinness. One by one, old age tells all of women's secrets.

"Mother always told me to learn to type," Stella watches a cowboy walk by outside. "Study Shorthand, she said, go to work in the office."

"Well, she probably told you right," Betty cranes her neck as if she might be watching a customer reach into her register.

"I don't know, to tell you the truth," says Stella, "Sometimes I think all I really do is dream. Dream about things."

Betty lights a cigarette and stands surveying Stella curiously through a cloud of smoke. Two gay guys go out the wrong door together. Stella hadn't noticed that they came in together, or that they came in at all, for that matter. Obviously, they met up inside. No doubt, they simply materialized somehow between the angry and the kitchen. Most likely, they sneaked in with the crowd, then left without them.

Next door, the music has disintegrated to a type of jungle rock-gone-rap. The wine, the imagined cigarette, the coffee all run together as people suddenly flip claim checks at her like confetti. For a moment she thinks it might be New Year's Eve. She believes she has truly endured the race and won the prize that people get when they make it all the way through their lives. The phone lines blink like Christmas tree lights. A drunk lady falls up the stairs, spills her portable drink then carelessly steps over the mess and bangs out into the cold night air. Laughter grows more urgent in the adjoining club while the music continues to prostitute its allegiance.

"Hon, you'll be alright," Betty's voice sounds way back as if in a fog.

The crowd thins with the thinning of her vision, and the proud claimee of the grey tweed hat steps forward, "Little lady, you did a fine job," he plops the hat squarely over his balding head, "here's this," he stuffs a five-dollar bill into the fat jar sitting on the cubicle ledge. Stella watches him, continues to watch outside where he grips his coat collar closer and slips on matching gloves. She finds it odd that he would check his hat and not his coat and gloves. She sees only him in the street now. He glances left and right, but there are no street people, there are no staggering drunks. She scans past the sign hanging on the closed door that opens into the hat check cubicle and reads as if for the first time: NOT RESPONSIBLE FOR ARTICLES LOST OR STOLEN. She points to the sign and addresses Betty, "Look at that, she says, "that's education enough, wouldn't you say?"

Betty offers no reply, but stares out onto the street, the remnants of her cigarette an ash on stub, while outside, cold curls like steam on a cloudless night.

THE COVID WALK

If I weren't sitting on the couch watching TV, I'd swear I was a journalist out there on the front lines shoving a microphone into people's faces and demanding, "How do you feel about inmates being forced to steep in their own Petri dishes?" If the person I was interviewing dared to lower their head and reply, "Excuse me?" I don't think I would have a satisfactory rebuttal ready. The virus rules, and there isn't much room for negotiation.

It's pretty bad when I have to hide my last two rolls of toilet paper from the piano tuner so he doesn't get any funny ideas. He hasn't actually asked to use the bathroom yet, and maybe he won't. But, before I take my morning walk and leave him alone in the house to tune the piano (his stipulation before committing was that I be gone while he was in the house to tune during this, the time of COVID), I'm not taking any chances. I fought too hard to get this toilet paper because all of the stores are perpetually out of toilet paper. They are actually out of a lot of things, but nothing really substitutes for toilet paper.

We had an outdoor toilet in Oklahoma, where I grew up, which was normal to me. It was a cute little house, a two-seater, very upscale for an outdoor toilet. But then, I've always loved houses and might have adopted the outdoor toilet as just another playhouse, except it smelled too bad, especially in the summer. You just did your thing, slammed the door, and walked back into the house. As for toilet paper, I can't remember what we used back then. I've heard jokes about the Sears catalog, but I can assure you that the Sears catalog was practically a bible at our house. It held a very prominent place on our coffee table where it sat for months, dog-eared and fettered, until the new one arrived in the mailbox. Then, possibly it got recycled to the outhouse. I don't remember

The piano tuner is coming today because I need a new diversion. I've had to fire the television after watching poor Governor Cuomo of New York, broadcasting daily from a warehouse, guiding frightened citizens like me as to the daily progression of the virus and the climbing death toll, which in the scheme of things is so frightening that if the piano tuner did actually steal my last two rolls of toilet paper while I was out walking, giving him his virus-free breathing space, I would find a way to cope. Possibly.

"They are sending us 400 ventilators," Governor Cuomo said on television. "Really?" he continued, "What am I going to do with 400 ventilators when I need 30,000 ventilators!" He looked to the right and to the left as he spoke, and although I could see nothing to the right and left of him, he was probably addressing news reporters while social distancing.

"Tell you what!" he continued, "YOU decide which of the 26,000 people left without a ventilator gets to live and who dies!" Governor Cuomo cannot hide his concern. He cares about each one of those New Yorkers on his watch. But I can see he is more desperate than angry.

I've never known a scare like this one. I worked right through SARS and H1N1. Back then, I never stopped working long enough to turn on the television, I guess. Equally, during the great wealth-swap of 2008, I was oblivious and miraculously untouched by the financial devastation of millions of homeowners. Again, too busy working, I was. But, this! We don't even know how to react. We have begun to turn on each other, to shout at one another, to hoard toilet paper, and to possibly steal the last two rolls left on earth.

Just before turning off the television and scheduling the piano tuner, I caught a scene of ice skaters in New York at Rockefeller Center. There weren't many of them; in fact, there were a whole lot fewer than I saw that year we visited New York. We had gone to Greenwich Village, and a passerby took a picture of us with our cell phone as we posed in front of a beautifully graffiti-painted mural. Then, later still in Greenwich Village, I bought a Vogue Original dress at the thrift store that benefits the homeless of New York.

The piano tuner is here, so I'll begin my daily walk. On these walks, I compare myself to a true-life television story I once saw of Holocaust survivors who lived underground in sewers for years. I, too, would be able to ration food and keep up my spirits just like they did. No problem. I would entertain myself in the sewers along with all of the other survivors by creating poetry, singing songs, and keeping a diary of the experience.

In the movie, when help came for those survivors after the end of their hiding in the sewers, the people were thin and extremely pale, almost Albino-like, and they were nearly blind, due to sunlight deprivation. But their faces registered such joy at feeling the wind on their faces and at seeing through their partially blind eyes the somewhat faded green of the trees. Although I am locked down, afraid to go to places, I can still stroll the sidewalks in early mornings, where I can usually be relatively certain not to see anyone, and the sun can still find my face. I will walk for miles and miles until the piano tuner texts me to come back home, that he is finished, and I should pay.

Usually, there is no one on the street when I walk. I walk

alone. The city is so deserted that I can take pictures on my phone and post them for friends to see, and people can post emojis of crying faces or of horrified faces. Besides, what few random people I shall see on these walks might become more and more frightening-looking with their masks and shields and gloves and hats. But I'll still walk with my stringy hair, wearing only sunglasses. Besides, I can take a different path and walk toward the locked-down strip mall, can gaze into store windows, and memorize the names of the jewelry I'll buy once COVID is over. Then, after walking past empty downtown stores, I'll cross the street and walk along the bay of the Atlantic Ocean to gaze out onto houseboats parked in the bay, where I still marvel at people who can hole up in something as small as a houseboat at a time like this. Those are the true survivors, them and the Holocaust survivors.

It is certain that soon I shall begin to see more people and more traffic because, frankly, it has become boring to continue to see closed stores with the same jewelry displays day after day. Besides, maybe I shall never again have a place to wear jewelry. Truthfully, food and toilet paper have become more important. Overall, aside from some phone conversations with friends, life has become more inward daily, more focused on raking leaves or pulling weeds, or on capturing spiders and moths inside the house and turning them outside where they can fly away free. This death toll has taken enough; therefore, it becomes more urgent to save all semblances of life.

How uncanny that, without me realizing it, my world has reduced itself to that box of a television where it seems there is a human connection. Like clockwork, those newscasters show up daily for me, giving me progress reports. They are still there somewhere, those newscasters. Rather than traffic or early morning walkers, my world has become far too spoon-fed via their priority, but it's the third month, and I can take no more. Soon, I will be forced to venture into the grocery store for fresh food. If it gets too desperate, I'll order something from Target. I'll launch a full-fledged campaign to boycott Amazon and Walmart so that when the virus disappears, I'll have a store to enter and browse.

I'll become more friendly with the birds, little song machines that once had been drowned by traffic noise. I'll feed the birds a mixture of drained hamburger grease mixed with dry oatmeal, and set it out in the mornings on the sidewalk beside the Crepe Myrtles. I'll fill their birdbaths with water and hang sweet, red sugar-water for the hummingbirds, positioning the feeders in low-hanging tree branches.

There is a hill I have to climb on my walk, which, though difficult at first, is becoming easier. I try distracting myself by adding up mail-box numbers and applying their numbers to their destiny assigned by Numerology. Sometimes that activity alone works wonders to distract me from the difficulty of climbing the hill.

If I do happen to see people coming toward me on the street, I'm the first to cross the street, which probably has a darker meaning, but I like to think it is because I'm a nice person. No matter the reason, it pays to cross the street if it means keeping the Virus at bay and out of my lungs for six months now, since I have resisted walking within ten feet of anyone, except, of course, the piano tuner.

People leave lots of furniture on the street, I notice. It's almost as if they are moving furniture outside so they can move more people inside.

Come inside. Lock the door, and the virus cannot reach you. That sounds like a dangerous idea, though. At least it does to me. And it is downright odd how one's idea of furniture changes all because of the pandemic. There might have been a time when I would have picked the furniture up, would have run to the house, and driven my car back to the curb, would have hauled the piece into the car, not caring if it scratched my dash or not. It's furniture! Today, however, I can sense the germs and viruses swarming all over the furniture like fish in a tidal wave, and I cross the street in disgust.

For several days now, when I've passed the bus stop, I read the big red sign that says, "Bus Closure Due to COVID." As a matter of fact, the buses haven't been running since March, and it is now September. I suppose everyone would be forced to walk there if there were really a place to go. Reading signs is only one way to shorten the walk. I also look for small walking entertainment things to do when the air feels heavy in my lungs, or is the Virus creeping into my lungs, insidious and quiet like the vacant streets? Temporarily, I breathe through my mouth, but the cool air makes my teeth hurt, so I stop that and resume nose-breathing.

Soon, it will begin the Feast of Tabernacles, the Festival of Shelters, the Feast of Ingathering, a biblical Jewish Holiday celebrated in the Book of Exodus, the end of harvest time and thus of the agricultural year. The Orthodox Jews will begin to set up their shelters built in the front yard of their houses, where they will sit outside at dusk and eat dinner. Quite the harvest we have had this year, though I strive to remain non-cynical. Besides, the piano tuner should be texting me any moment that he has finished, and that it is safe to return to the house.

I am nearing the steep hill where I must take a deep breath and walk fast to climb with full breath before reaching and then coming down. I think of a time when I will visit the mall again, and go shopping with friends, because when women go shopping, they like to talk about the clothes they bought the last time they went shopping together: "I got this the last time we went shopping together," she would say. And I would say, "It looked much better on you than it did on the hanger." And she would say, "Thank you."

As if channeling Edgar Allan Poe, a black crow flies low into the turn lane on the street and stops while a lone car approaches. Then, the crow disappears into trees across the street, which tree limb hangs over the sides of the road, growing toward the sun, some more brown than others, faring the Fall weather in different degrees, some more, some less successfully, like people. Even the grass is two shades of green – class distinctions even in nature. One day soon, these COVID sidewalks will scramble for leftover pieces of information, or insight, of any thread of knowledge of what went wrong.

When I left the house right after the piano tuner arrived, I swabbed my nostrils with an antibiotic cream in order to defy airborne viruses, to bid them die if they accidentally infiltrated my automatic breaths. The viruses are invisible, they say, unlike the reminders littering the sidewalks of furniture, of discarded masks, and of small, empty, used-up bottles of hand sanitizer.

On the last leg of the COVID Walk, I see that police cars block the road ahead. Has there been a death? A murder? There are electrical lights on the ground, and there is an ambulance. Has someone fallen down the other side of the steep hill? Should I cross the street?

No, I'll continue steadily back toward the house when the piano man texts, but before paying him, I'll quickly check the bathroom, and if all is still not well, if he has taken the toilet paper, I'll merely give the police his license plate number.

IN HONOR OF MOZART

I thought about it for several days before I decided that Jenny was the one person to whom I would disclose the fact that I think I had fallen in love. I would confess it over lunch. Besides, I hadn't seen much of her lately, and I know as well as anyone that innocent neglect is how friends lose touch.

Jenny Giles, my best friend, was also my closest confidant. She was also a topless dancer, a classically trained ballerina, and Mike Gowan's girlfriend. Her appeal at this moment lay in her sheer ability to unclutter most things. If I needed to mull over my new love interest, she was the perfect one to either set me straight or at least to lend a neutral listening ear. Basic and simple, easily distracted, she had not yet developed the annoying habit some people have of laboring a point too long. Unlike most of my current friends, acquaintances, or family members, who provide an ongoing sort of academic suffocation, Jenny would gracefully relinquish with no tiresome back talk, any comment I might immediately wish to retract. I needed that freedom at a time like this.

Another reason that she seemed to be the ideal sounding board was that I would be free to expound, and she would accept any contradiction, any extravagance, any flight of fantasy with little demand for sanity. Love dissection requires this frame of mind. Having repeatedly failed her attempts to make the Debate Team in college because of her congenital indifference to logic, she had nevertheless managed to maintain the fluidity of an ocean (which could just as easily flow in opposite directions simultaneously) because she had a knack, an absolute knack, for listening more to the rhythm than the notes.

Every generality has its exception, of course, and if Jenny had one, it was that where Mike was concerned, nothing escaped her. Once at the club where she danced, she slugged a guy for 'coming onto Mike.'

I dialed her number and she answered on the first ring, as if she had been sitting by the phone waiting for a call.

"Jenny, hey, it's me..Chris," I said.

She sounded surprised to hear from me, then excited, "H-i-e-e-e. How are you-u? How've you been? I was going to c-a-l-l you," she gushed.

"I'm fine. Wonderful, in fact," I decided against simply launching right into the subject of my new boyfriend. "I haven't talked to you in so long. Guess I've been busy," I said, giving a build-up to the event soon to be announced. "What you been up to?" I asked.

"I-e-e, well, I have been waiting for…truthfully, I thought you might be one of those ridiculous l-a-d-i-e-s who are supposed to call me back," her voice sounded small.

"What ladies?" I asked, "Oh, were you expecting another call? I can call back later," I said.

"No. I mean, yes! But, how are y-o-u?" she shouted into the phone.

"Like I said, I'm doing great. I thought I'd see if you would like to have lunch today. I have something that I want to run by you," I said, grossly downplaying the situation.

She hesitated, thinking, "I'd love to, but... I have this... well, actually, I've been sitting here thinking if I should call you. Isn't that crazy-e-e?" Jenny had this way, like a singer, of holding onto words as if singing vowels.

"Telepathy, maybe," I said.

"Oh, I don't know. Maybe. But, I have this problem, and I'm really worried," she said.

"What? What kind of problem?" I asked, knowing full well that what Jen called a problem and what really proved to be a problem might be in no way related.

"Yeah," she said, "I'm supposed to get a dog today. A puppy," she truly sounded worried.

"That doesn't sound like a problem to me," I said. "That sounds like a happy occasion."

"It is h-a-p-p-y-e-e," she brightened, "except these ladies are so w-e-i-r-d!"

"Weird? What do you mean weird?" I had a vision of some blackmarket operation in the offing, some undercover dog processing operation, and I knew how Jen felt about animals.

"Well, rude-weird," she said.

"Wait a minute," I said, "Did you say they were weird or rude?" I asked. "Both!" she said.

'They are rude because they asked me-e-e all these dumb questions."

"Like what?" I asked.

"And, they are weird," she continued, "because even though he is going to be m-y-i-i- dog… five hundred bucks worth… they want to tell me what to n-a-m-e-e- him!"

"Yeah," I agreed, "that IS weird. Why are they rude?"

"Because," she said, as if I should already know the answer, "they are asking me all kinds of q-u-e-s-t-i-o-n-s about me! Like what is my vet's name, and, oh, I don't know.. I'm just so n-e-r-v-o-u-s."

"That is a little ridiculous," I was beginning to wonder if we should make lunch another day. After all, there would be plenty of time for me to tell her about Keith. Of this, I felt fairly certain.

"Now, I'm thinking, what if they won't let me h-a-v-e him?" she said.

"Why wouldn't they, for heaven's sake? It isn't as if they are GIVING him away," I said, "You ARE paying them $500, I believe I heard you say."

"I know," her voice trailed up, "It isn't as if I don't know a d-a-m-n thing about dogs. I've always had dogs. I know how to care for them. I'm a farm girl for Pete's sake!" Then she seemed to breathe a sigh of relief as she continued, "Chris, you should see 'em."

I wondered if she meant the ladies or the dog, but she continued, "He's so beautiful! He's a St. Bernard p-u-p-p-y. I want him so bad." She was silent for a moment. "Could you help me?"

By now, I had pretty much abandoned my idea for a declaration, mainly because it no longer seemed important; her dilemma seemed much more immediate. "Certainly, I will help. What can I do?" I asked.

"Can I pick you up from work? Maybe if they see YOU they won't ask me so many stupid q-u-e-s-t-i-o-n-s!" she said.

I couldn't quite figure that one out, but knowing Jen, I reasoned there must have been some mutant form of logic at work here, so I asked, "What exactly can I do? I mean, is this going to take longer than an hour? I will be, you know, on my lunch hour," I said.

"Oh, no. They're probably on their way over her right now. I think I can pick you up and be back here by the t-i-m-e they get here. Meet me in the lobby downstairs, okay?" She hung up the receiver just as I was saying 'bye', so I began to shift papers around on my desk, put my answering machine on message, and just in case I got detained, I asked Max if he could dock me for an hour since I had to run an errand at lunch.

She picked me up in the lobby of the office building and told me the situation as we drove to her apartment. It was very simple. She was buying an extremely well-bred dog, and the owners were reluctant to entrust the dog to an incompetent owner. Money, in cases such as this one, was not the only consideration.

The weather was beginning to spit freezing ice onto the roads, but she grew impatient with drivers poking along ahead of her and testily buzzed around them. Riding in any moving vehicle in weather such as this unnerved me. She knew it and laughed, "Poor baby," she displayed a wide expanse of teeth, "We'll get there, don't worry." She stared out the window and paid closer attention to the road. "I like nasty weather, I really do."

"I knew it!" I had long suspected there were those who griped about the weather only because it sounded fashionable. "Somewhere in the world, there truly ARE people like you who enjoy hazardous weather."

"Most idiots don't know how to drive in it, though. Look at him!" She beeped her horn and passed a guy who was doing about 10 miles an hour. She looked over her shoulder at him as she passed, and continued a while looking in the rear-view mirror instead of at the road. For a moment, I was afraid she was going to throw him an obscene gesture; however, she soon looked back at the road.

"Do you know, Jen, I have actually embarrassed myself calling off at work sometimes to tell them I couldn't make it and then found out that everyone else made it in fine," I confessed.

She smiled, but it was obvious she was preoccupied with her problem, while her driving was largely instinctive. "Chris, I am so nervous about these ladies," she said.

"I don't understand why," I said.

"They are so.." she pressed her lips into a tight line and made a mock saccharine smile, "you know. Plus they asked me all these q-u-e-s- t-i-o-n-s!"

"Like what kind of questions?" I swayed in my seat as we hit another patch of ice and skidded slightly.

"They almost insulted me. Asked what my mother thinks of me having a show dog. What the hell does my MOTHER have to do with anything? I don't live at home. Why did they ask me that?"

"Well," I said, "You do look kind of young. Maybe they thought you still lived at home." I said. "Or, maybe," I continued, "maybe they were just trying to feel you out on the subject. You know how they probably feel, having those quality dogs." I didn't know a bloody thing about dogs, really, except that they require love, attention, and time out of your life for something other than yourself.

Her eyes lit and shone with an inner fever, "Wait 'til you see 'em. He's a big baby. He weighs about 40 pounds already."

She had sped up her driving to match the excitement of the subject, but slowed down again and continued, "Oh, and another thing. I want to name him Wolfie," her voice rose into a question mark, "in honor of Mozart?" She looked at me and continued, "You know Wolfgang Amadeus Mozart." She studied my reaction. "You know him, don't you?"

"I think that's a pretty classy name myself," I said. "Of course, I know who Mozart was."

"They want me to name him Chester!" she said with an exclamation of disgust.

"You mean they even have the name picked out for the dog they are selling you?" I was beginning to understand the gravity of the situation now.

"That's why I am afraid I might not get 'em," she said. "Don't tell them I'm going to name 'em.." she trailed off.

"Why didn't you just say you intended to name him Fang and hang up in their ear?" I said.

Her hands tightened on the steering wheel. "How can I tell them I'm not naming him Chester? Oh," she shook the steering wheel," I'm so nervous."

"Don't tell them anything. Or, just SAY you are going to name him Chester, then do what you damn well please. What difference does it make to them what you name your dog?" I asked.

"Well, they have this... Oh, I don't know," her voice faded again.

"Don't worry, you'll do fine," I said. It was difficult for me to comprehend how she could maneuver like an expert over treacherous ice and snow, yet fret so much over chronic dowager-ism.

"And, you know what else? They asked me where he was going to sleep. I have always had dogs," she said. "Listen, I treat 'em good. And, I've saved my money. Five hundred cash. I don't think the ladies believed me," her eyes narrowed to a frowning stare. "Maybe that's it. She didn't think I had the money," she sounded surprised.

That was probably the situation. How could the ladies realize how much a topless dancer earned? They probably thought

Jen still lived at home or worked at McDonald's or something.

"Jen, just leave this to me," I assumed a false bravado even though I had no particular move in mind, but I felt she could use a little shot of confidence at this point. "I'll handle those old bats."

She laughed, her eyes slits, an excited child, and beat the steering wheel in celebrated anticipation, "He is the biggest of the bunch. He'll get about 200 pounds."

"Good heavens, Jen," I had never understood the fascination some people had for big dogs, but Jen was tall, and she would look good walking a St. Bernard. She stood with perfect posture always, probably a habit acquired from years and years of studying ballet. At times when she caught herself slumping, she would deliberately straighten, thrusting forward her hips, rolling her torso straight, and aligning her head with an imaginary string suspended from the ceiling. Then, she would tuck in her tummy and shake her head, shaking also her hair, which streamed straight down her back to just below her waist.

"They're even bringing food. I have to feed him puppy food at first. Wait until you see my baby," she was looking at me, smiling widely, her eyes slits on high cheekbones.

We arrived at her apartment about five minutes before they came. She asked me to pretend that the poodle her mother left there was mine for the time being. In fact, she even asked if I wanted to buy it. But, as it was not yet house-trained, I said no.

A van pulled up in the outside driveway, and we watched

from the window. Two pudgy, middle-aged ladies got out, one holding the leash on one of the most gorgeous St. Bernard pups I had ever seen. Jen let out an excited, "E-e-e."

I could see what she meant: everything about the women looked fussy. They obviously took their dog breeding very seriously. One woman held in one hand what looked to be a picture album, and a big sack of puppy food in the other. The shorter, blonde woman guided the dog by a leash. He kept shaking his head, his ears elaborately bandaged and tied, and she bent over him to straighten something on his bandage.

"What's wrong with his ears?" I asked Jen.

"They're tied up so they will grow straight up," she said, "I'm going to SHOW that little baby!"

They walked up to the door and rang the doorbell. Jen motioned quickly to me, "You answer it. I am going to get my money. And, remember…" she made a gesture with her hands, and along with the grimace on her face, I interpreted it to mean: 'Act Intelligent.' So, I tried.

"Hello. Come in," I said in as snooty a manner as I could muster.

The little black poodle came running into the living room and started to bark. I remembered I didn't even know his name, and that he was supposed to be mine, so I picked him up while he growled at me the entire time, so I began to scratch behind his ears to calm him down.

The taller lady, obviously well-versed in social dog-ology, grinned at him, "Oh, isn't he cute?" She touched his nose, and he sniffed her hands suspiciously, then began to bark at the big dog.

"Hush," I said to him, and to the lady I said, "Let me go put him in the back room. He has never seen another dog before."

"Oh?" she answered, raising her eyebrows in surprise.

"Not one that big, anyway," I walked down the hall, put the poodle in the bathroom, and shut the door. He began really barking now, barking and scratching at the bathroom door like crazy. In all fairness, and Jen knows this, I am not wild about dogs, or any pets for that matter. There is a pretty good reason for this, and it is all tied up with having my kitten die on me once. However, I won't go into that now.

I walked back into the living room, still trying to act intelligent and half-way presentable, "Ladies, please sit down."

Jen entered the room with a handful of money. She sat down on the nearest chair and started spreading the money out. She had adopted a somewhat formal air, for her, as she continued in silence to sort fives, tens, and twenties into separate stacks. There was something almost obscene about watching her count out $500 in cash. I don't know, and I think I was merely picking up on the blonde lady's brain waves, but people usually write checks or charge something that costs $500.

I decided to do my bit, and extending my hand to the lady nearest me, I said, "I'm Chris."

"Hi," she said, taking my hand. "I'm Vera, this is my sister, Louise. Do you girls work together?" she asked.

"Actually," I said, applying a trace of a British accent to my first word, "we attended college together. We became friends in Algebra," I lied.

"Oh!" Vera seemed delighted. I figured Algebra would impress her. There seems to be something consistent with the older generation and their unanimous trust in left-brained, more tangible undertakings.

Louise turned and spoke to Jen, who now had four large stacks of money in neat piles, "We brought you a picture album of his baby pictures. Have you decided on his name yet?" They really WERE after that name thing.

"U-m," Jen looked at me, "Yeah, I thought…"

"She really rather liked your idea of naming him Chester," I applied the British accent as I lied again.

"Well, something English, you know, would be preferable," said Louise.

Jen wrinkled her nose in disgust, "Chester? He looks more Indian to me than English," she said.

"Oh, but darling," said Vera, "his name is English. He looks, of course, like a St. Bernard."

I waved the air, "We shall decide very soon. And, when we decide, you'll be the first to know," I said.

"Yes, please," said Louise, "when you decide, let us know. We're keeping a family history of all of his descendants, and we would like to keep it, to enter his name on the family tree," she began searching through the picture album, "somewhere

here…I brought his family tree…here it is."

This was really more involved than I would have ever imagined. Ashamed of myself, I began to wonder if maybe they weren't making a mistake after all, entrusting this dog with all his genealogical baggage to Jen.

Louise, who had now located the family history, began to point out various names and facts on a sheet of paper that looked very much like a synopsis of the stock market for the past 10 years.

"We checked with your Vet, and he gave us very good references," Louise said, pleased with her efficiency.

Jen reddened a bit, and I could see her mouth tighten, but she managed a smile, "I'm glad he did."

Louise continued, "We certainly are going to miss Chester."

I began to actually feel sorry for Vera and Louise as I watched Jen hand them the money. Seeming to be done with their friendly chatter, Jen asked, "Will he get real big?"

"Yes, in fact, you are going to have to watch him. He eats too much, and he's lazy," said Vera.

"Don't worry," said Jen, "I plan to exercise him." She bent down and offered him pursed lips as she talked, "he is going to run with me every day."

"Well," persisted Louise, "Not too much exercise, you don't want his bones to grow too fast."

Jen looked at her dryly, "I know."

While they finished up with formalities, I slipped down the hall toward the bathroom where I had stashed the poodle. He was quiet now. I bent down and looked at the bottom of the door. I could hear him sniff loudly, and could see his shadow playing back and forth just underneath the door. For one crazy moment, I toyed with the idea of taking him home with me. His presence in my life would certainly be something new. It would be a stab at commitment, something maybe I should try before I settle in with the new love in my life. As I stretched my legs out on the wood floor in front of the bathroom and leaned my head back against the door, I was suddenly unsure if I was ready for commitment of any kind. I had never put much thought into the steps I took, but just took them and let fate decide the outcome. This dog thing, I decided, might just be nothing short of an omen.

FAIRY TALES

Her mother read her stories. When alone in her room, the girl played records. She played the songs over and over until she had them memorized…

sing a song of sixpence
pocket full of rye

frosty the snowman was a happy jolly soul

buffalo gals won't you come out tonight,
come out tonight,
come out tonight

The songs and the stories were rich and full: castles set against clear, blue sky and lush green woods stacked richly against her barren Midwestern plains, where turbulent winds often rattled winter windows.

One day, she walked across the street to see if Scott wanted to play prince and princess. Often, he did. He would tie a bath towel around his neck and let it flap in the wind like a cape. His baseball bat became a sword because he never played baseball with the bat anyway. On those days when they played prince and princess, Bonnie would wear her Mother's glittery earring and red pop beads, and tie a silky scarf around her head.

She stepped up onto the porch and carefully clamped the earrings on her ears. It was important not to put them on too soon because after about 15 minutes, they began to pinch and sting her ears. She slipped the beads around her neck and looked down at them. They hung long and rich, striking about the waist. She moved from side to side to watch how the beads moved gracefully back and forth over the tiny flowers on her dress. She held the long scarf from her hand and waved it high above her head, watching its graceful billow in the morning breeze like a purple frilly flag at half-mast. Then she knocked, full-fisted at Scott's front door.

Her small hand rapping at the massive wooden door created a shallow tap. She knocked harder and waited. She looked up at the wooden overhang on the porch, then pressed her ear against the door and listened for sounds of the family within. Her ear against the door created a roaring sound like water crashing in a seashell. She listened for human thumps or voices, but heard nothing. Clearly, Scott was not home. She backed up to the edge of the porch, turned around, and sat down on the top step to wait for him. She could hear morning birds chirping in trees above, and the sun was at the correct angle to stare her straight in the eye. Suddenly, she felt all alone and deserted, like Goldilocks. How could Scott not be home? Also, the roar of the prairie wind sounded like bears out there. Bears were in the woods. She jumped up, turned back toward the large door, and ran straight to it. She leaned her cheek against the door. The wood felt warm now, so she reached up to the large brass doorknob and turned it. The door creaked, then opened, and she stood in a sunbathed room with white curtains flowing from opened windows.

"Hello. Is anyone home? Goldilocks has come to see you, Scott. She is lonely from home," she yelled into the kitchen.

The room stood silent, yet welcoming. She stepped a few feet across the dark wooden floor and onto the green rug that sat in front of the fireplace. Before her stretched the room, the fireplace was flanked by two large chairs, one with a round ottoman sitting in front of it. Slowly, she walked toward the tallest chair. Gliding with deliberate cadence to the tune of an imaginary waltz, she reverently approached the tall chair. She crawled up into the chair and sat down. She raised her hands to rest them on the arms of the big chair. Leaning her head back against the coarse upholstery, she closed her eyes and said, "Ooh, this chair is too hard."

After resting there for a minute, she looked again around the room. The white curtain blew into the room as if to say, Try... try another chair. She jumped down out of the large chair and walked around the ottoman to crawl up into the other chair. She scooted way back, deeply into the chair, pointing both feet straight in front of her, toes pointed like a Ballerina, and said, 'And... this chair is too soft.' Turning on her stomach in the chair, she hopped down backwards, which put her sitting exactly squarely on the overstuffed ottoman. She lay back on the ottoman and let her head hang back as she surveyed the room from that upside-down vantage point. She imagined what it would feel like to walk around on the ceiling. There was no furniture up there, so there would be lots of room to walk around. All she would have to do would be to remember to step over the light fixture. In awe of that consideration, she raised herself, hair following tidily up her back as she came to a sitting position, and said, 'But this chair is just right!'

She rolled off the ottoman and lay on the green rug for a second. She could smell dust and fiber, "Scott, I wish you were home so we could play prince and princess."

The house creaked as if to answer her. Was someone there? Maybe it was a mouse. It was Spring, and maybe all the field mice had not yet left the warmth of the house. She hopped up and began to walk straight into the kitchen. The kitchen floor had big squares of blue linoleum on it. One rainy day, Scott's mother had let them draw with white chalk, lines around the squares, and play hopscotch in the house.

A red chrome dinette set of table and 6 chairs dominated the center of the kitchen. White glass-fronted cabinets hung on the walls. She walked towards the cabinets and tried to open a door, but the cabinets were too high up. She couldn't reach them, so she decided to open and play in the cabinets nearest the floor. She could sit on the floor and do that.

Behind most of the doors were pots and pans and boxes of brightly colored cans. Behind the tall door, she spied large colored mixing bowls. She reached in to pick them up, but stacked together, they were heavy, so she reached inside the stack and retrieved the smallest bowl, a yellow one with a white stripe around the rim. She set it to the far right side of her, then changed her mind and picked it up again, and, carrying it to the table, she scooted it onto the edge81of the table. That done, she walked back to the cabinet, picked up the second bowl, a slightly larger bowl, this time green with a white stripe, and placed it on the other end of the table. She walked back to pick up the biggest bowl, but halfway there she heard a sound bigger than a mouse and louder than the wind. She listened again and heard her name, "B-o-n-n-i-e.." She stood very still and held her breath, but she heard it again, this time louder and more insistent, "Bonnie, where are you?"

"BONNIE," her mother was now calling in that irritated tone of voice. She paused with the bowl in mid-air, aware for the first time that the earrings were really digging into her ears. She set the bowl down on the floor and squatted while she pulled off first one earring, then the other.

'This porridge is too hot,' she said as she dipped her finger into the imaginary soup in the first bowl. "Bonnie, time to come home now," her mother's voice seemed to be getting either louder or closer. She sat down on the cool floor and carefully placed the earrings in the large bowl.

She looked up to see a drawer that probably held the silverware she needed to eat the porridge, but decided it might be too high to reach, so she stood and walked towards the red vinyl chair, "B-o-n-n-i-e!"

The music swelling louder than the yelling, she walked past the chair and began to waltz towards the front door. At the archway leading from the kitchen, she stopped and strapped the silk scarf around her waist. Then, she waltzed and swayed, trailing the stream of scarf behind her outside into the midday breeze.

* *

"There is an innocence about you," he says, "that I absolutely adore."

She looks at his face sideways because straight on, his face often looks blurry, "You think so?" she asks.

"A sexual innocence, too," he says.

She looks at a place on the floor, knowing he is arbitrarily discounting every man in her past, as maybe he should. The music from the radio has become so progressively atonal that they could very easily be sitting in a spaceship ready for takeoff.

"I've never had this before," he says as he lights a cigarette.

Don't, she thinks. Don't say it. Don't think you have to. Especially, don't say it if you think you have to. She almost says this out loud, but the words, soft in her head, will come out harshly, and she knows it, so she says nothing. Talk is cheap anyway, and everywhere there are lovers who tell themselves anything. Cheap lovers are everywhere. She is almost disappointed that he has chosen a subject other than the stock market or the upcoming Presidential election.

"It is as Socrates said," he continues, "Maybe it was Plato… not sure." He stares straight ahead, chin raised in thought, cigarette now extinguished, but puffs of smoke lingering around them like blue protoplasm.

"Most of the time," she interrupts, "I think we…"

He turns to look at her, his back bent in front of her, her breasts pressed against him, "Yes?" he anticipates.

"I think we take a long time, make a lot of mistakes, and then either figure it out or just give up on it," she says.

"Well, that sounds a bit jaded," he says, "but, yeah, maybe."

Hands slide up to his shoulders, she pushes away slightly, and begins to softly scratch his back. He bends down, arching his back like a cat rising to meet each stroke. She glides over freckles, resting her head on his left shoulder as the music issues into the night, odder than ever.

"Mother always used to maintain that she read me too many fairy tales," she attempts to explain away any ill-perceived, unearned innocence.

He stretches out on the bed on his stomach, back facing upward, while she continues to scratch.

"I even used to act them out when I was a child," she continues.

"Ahah," he says, "once an actress, always an actress!"

"Could be," she says, "Once I pretended to be Goldilocks, and I went into the neighbor's house to do all the things Goldilocks did with the three bears. I sat on chairs, tasted porridge, and lay on the beds. No, I didn't actually get to that part."
"Seriously?" He raises to a sitting position and looks at her, "How did you do that?" he asks, amazed.

"One has ways when one has imagination," she says. She gets off the bed and goes into the bathroom. "You know, I really don't like this time of day," she says.

He looks out the window at the disappearing sun. Once he had told her that Twilight was his favorite time of day. "Why not?" he asks.

"Depresses me," she calls from behind the closed bathroom door. Then, opening the door, she comes out and walks back toward the bed, "Not to plagiarize Hemingway or anything, but I really believe when I die it will be at Twilight."

"God forbid," he says and reaches his arms straight toward her. She sits again beside him on the bed, "Don't be a dope," he says.

Outside, hummingbirds have taken to their nest in the trees as the sun makes its way carefully past the horizon and the radio music travails on. Night safely settled in, she knows she is safe one more day.

GREEN CARS

Joyce wakes late in the morning to find she is lying in a fine mist of perspiration. Through her bedroom window, an eastern exposure, the sun peeps through shutter slats and casts straight lines of alternate shade and sun onto her new flowered comforter that is mostly a white background with tiny lavender flowers sprinkled sparsely. She has left the nightlight burning in the hall near the bathroom, and its glow, so vivid in the dark of night, is now subdued enough by the sun's competition as to have become invisible.

She opens her eyes to the invading rays, squinting back at them, and considers the meaning of the dream she has just had, a recurring dream of a black piano that moves in each dream from one room to another.

The setting for the first dream was inside a large castle, very dark, where an unhappy maiden lived who despite her unhappiness was still plagued with the task of disposing of an extra black piano, the black piano in the dream. It seems that in addition to the two black pianos, the maiden had also acquired a large white pipe organ that wrapped around an entire room, its pipes extending so high upwards to the ceiling that there was some question as to whether holes might need to be cut into the ceiling to properly accommodate the lengthy pipes.

But the true dilemma in the dream appeared to be not the process of carving up the ceiling, but appeared to be the issue of whether to, or whether not to, discard the extra black piano which had now become a thing of excess. In these dreams, feelings surrounding the eviction of the black piano were those of sadness at having inadvertently having to replace it, along with an infantile desire to hold onto the outgrown object, and a suspicion of utter wastefulness at having willfully displaced a perfectly good and fully functioning musical instrument.

Perhaps Joyce dreams so vividly because she goes so often to the movies. There is some discussion as to whether movies activate the imagination or whether they nullify it; however, Joyce suspects the former to be true.

When Joyce attends the movies, she usually finds herself standing in long lines because rarely has she the patience to wait until a movie has been around long enough to digress to the cut-rate movie houses. Besides, there is a cleansing ritual associated with movie-going: the crowds, the drinks and popcorn, the overpriced candy. Every time she goes, she eats the same thing: a medium Coke, medium popcorn, and a Butterfinger candy bar.

As she stands in line, she studies the face of the latest starlet-hopeful gazing back from the movie poster on the wall. One day, if properly hoarded, this movie poster might be a valuable collectible to rival old Humphrey Bogart movie posters.

She buys her ticket and heads down the thickly carpeted hall towards a girl who stands in front of the ticket box, her hand held pre-functionally forward to seize the ticket, tear it in half, and deposit the stub into the final blackness of the box.

The ticket taker doesn't exactly smile, but she doesn't scowl either. Goaded by the boredom of a repetitious act in a faceless crowd, she wears the neutral face of a public servant who, to maintain within herself some form of sanctum, thinks about where she wants to go on her birthday and what she will wear.

Joyce looks at the ticket taker, but soon looks away and merely feels her half of the ticket stub being shoved into her hand. She pastes a small grimace on her face, the grimace, being directed more towards the array of movie posters aligning the wall, yet is still in place in case any live human being might be watching – a sort of gratis smile.

The theatre, mostly empty, is quiet and dim. Music plays over the speaker system, and masks of comedy and tragedy smile and frown from the floor carpeting. She chooses to sit rather far back and near the aisle, leaving only one seat to her right. She is near enough to the aisle that she can run out if absolutely necessary, yet the aisle seat gives her the illusion of company.

Three people walk in, and one whispers, "God, we are early. Where do you want to sit?"

She hears them chomp popcorn and rustle around, their seats plunking, until all is quiet again. She twiddles her hair, knowing a strand probably falls against the white cable knit sweater she is wearing. Leg draped across the back of the seat in front of her, she wonders if anyone in here recognizes her from her latest and most successful run ever of Summer and Smoke.

When she had auditioned for Summer and Smoke, 120 women had shown up at the audition, most of them vying for the part of Miss Alma. After narrowing the callbacks down to 4 women, one of them Joyce, the director conducted an interview wherein he asked her, "Why do you want to play Miss Alma?"

She had twirled her hair then very much as she was doing now, and the director had said, "Never mind. Stop right there.

I can see you are Miss Alma! You've got the part."

Crunching popcorn and talking of ordinary things, a young black couple walks into the theatre and sits two rows in front of Joyce. They go on talking about shoes and shoe sizes instead of how the leaves outside are turning a glorious gold against the dawn. She points her fingers together as if in prayer and feels fairly ecclesiastical sitting there in the theatre. Lately, she has been letting days run over her like a stream runs over rocks. On good days, she fantasizes she might grow moss or something. It is a new consideration, this sudden preoccupation with attempting to emulate the finest qualities of trees and snow. Possibly, she reasons, she has been studying too much method acting lately.

A stockily built male with curly hair and beard walks into the theatre and proceeds down the aisle. She looks at him and recognizes that he is a friend of her ex-husband, a friend neither of them has seen for a while.

"Psst, Russ," she whispers.

The man turns, looks in the direction of her seat, but his eyes, not yet acclimated to the dark, see nothing.

"Russell, over here. It's Joyce!" Russell frowns and squints in the dark, much as one might in bright sunlight. Dichotomies are maddening that way.

"Joyce?" he calls.

"Yeah, here, behind you," she raises her hand.

He sees her and begins to head back up the aisle. "How are

you, angel?" He shoves his sturdy frame into the lone seat next to her, "Long time no see."

"What are you doing here?" she asks.

"Same thing you are, I guess," he says.

"It's good to see you," she pats his arm.

"Same here," he says, "A nice surprise on a Wednesday afternoon. You don't have class today?"

"No, not on Wednesdays," she says. "You off work?"

"Uh-hum," he mumbles, "Temporarily permanently."

"What do you mean?" she asks.

"Temporary layoff," he says, "But I don't mind. I need the rest. I'll get something started up again."

"I'm sure," she says.

"How's Dave?" he asks.

"Well, you probably see him as much as I do," she squirms.

"Not really. I haven't seen anyone much lately," he volunteers.

"He's fine. We've become very good friends, actually. We have breakfast occasionally. We parted on good terms, though. He calls me sometimes," she says.

"That's great," Russel looks at the movie screen, "I'll have to call him."

The movie lights go down, and the sound comes up. Imaginary curtains part, and the lion's head roars, and soon the movie title begins. The movie is a love story, and she can tell that the actor and actress are not really acting. Later, she reads that they fell in love during the filming of the movie, actually lived together for a short time after the end of the filming, then parted.

After the movie is over, she and Russell walk out into the mall and stroll aimlessly with other Wednesday afternoon mall cruisers. They look at meaningless distractions, ceramic pumpkins smiling, garish from their department store displays. They walk past racks and racks of clothing, some sombre, some sparkling, and they walk on toward the Italian restaurant that is sandwiched between the US Postal Service and the Hallmark card shop down near the end of the mall.

"I like this place," Russell says as he eyes the restaurant's attempt at decor, a plastic string of onions hanging just inside the door.

"Do you want to stop in?" she asks.

Directly outside the restaurant, there are new Chevrolet cars on display in the mall behind ropes. She bends over to study her reflection in a shiny red car. The face is pretty, the hair stringy and loose.

"You know," she says to Russell, "red cars have more accidents than other colors of cars. I read statistics about all kinds of stupid stuff."

"I have read the same thing," he says, still looking inside the restaurant, "Something to do with either the aggressive people who buy red cars, or maybe it's the aggressive feeling other drivers get when they see red cars on the road. Like they just want to crash into them or something."

"Who knows," she says. "Weird. It's weird. Lots of stuff is weird."

"Hey, Joyce," Russell asks, "You hungry?"

"I had popcorn," she says, "but I could eat something, maybe a salad, a glass of wine."

"Let's do it," he says, and he walks into the restaurant, then walks up to the hostess, holding up two fingers. Joyce follows him.

The hostess places them near a window that looks out onto the street. The sky outside is dark, like skies can be when they threaten rain.

"That movie was pretty good," she tells Russell.

"Pretty good," he nods in agreement, "Pretty unrealistic."

"Unrealistic?" she asks, "Yeah, probably."

"I'm just feeling that way today," he says, "I'll probably look at it differently, I am sure, when the next woman comes into my life."

"No doubt," she says as she watches out the window another red car turn the corner with a squeal and speed out of sight.

"Did I mention that Dave and I had become pretty good friends since the divorce?" she asks.

"That's what you said," Russel replies.

"It's ironic," she looks outside and sees clouds churning, "Since we have been apart, I ask myself, was it really that bad? What was it that we couldn't seem to work out? I cannot seem to remember."

"That happens all the time," Russell scoots down and sprawls his legs into the aisle. The waitress nearly trips on them as she approaches the table. "Are you ready to order?" she asks.

Joyce looks again at the menu, and Russell points to an area in the upper quadrant of the middle section of the menu, "I'll have the mushroom Swiss with extra mayonnaise," he says. "Also, what kind of beer do you have on draft?"

The waitress shifts to her right foot and draws the order pad close to her, "We have Bud, Miller Lite, and Heineken."

"I'll have a Bud," he says.

"And you, ma'am," the waitress turns to Joyce.

"I'll have," she scans the menu one last time, "a spinach salad and Chablis, the house Chablis will be fine."

"Okay," the waitress writes fast.

"And, bring me a side of cheese bread," Joyce adds.

"Cheese bread," the waitress repeats as she writes. She turns again to Russell.

"Did you care for anything else? Appetizer? Soup?" she asks him.

"No," he hands her the menu, "That's all. We might have dessert," he winks at Joyce.

A spitting of rain begins to hit the window beside them, and as Joyce watches a raindrop trail down the glass like a baby liquid snake, she suddenly remembers a different part of the dream that woke her this morning.

In the dream, some people had commented on how the black piano she had placed on the front porch was getting wet from the rain. She knew that moisture was deadly to pianos, and for this reason the piano was very likely ruined by now. However, she believed in her heart that the piano would be okay, and she made a decision to move the piano back into the house. This she would do regardless of what anyone said, and she would nurture it back to health. In the dream, she knew the piano would crowd not only the other furniture, but also the other musical instruments in the house. She knows that the presence of an old, unwanted piano would even interfere with a certain balanced decor. But, she also suspected that in the long run, certain humanitarian considerations beat out convenience and beauty, hands down.

"I do believe," Russell says, "that had I taken time for counseling like Sue wanted to do, that we might still be married."

"Do you? Why?" Joyce notices that a couple at a nearby table is watching them.

"I would have been rid sooner of a lot of excess baggage," he pulls his legs back from the aisle.

Joyce nods in acknowledgement, fully understanding and mostly agreeing.

"Because, actually," he continues, "the problem of forming satisfactory relationships comes not from the crap we receive, but in how we choose to deal with it."

"I don't know what that says about me," Joyce thinks of how she had stuck with Dave when all else had deserted him.

"How is that?" Russell asks.

"I was a master at handling the crap, but I wasn't really coping," she watches a steady raindrop break apart on the window.

"You were just..." Russell says.

"Bottling things up," she volunteers. "Keeping score. That's not good."

"No, it's not," he says, "you can't do that. That never works."

"I know," she says.

"It's not really fair, when you think about it," he says.

"I know," she says.

"To you," he clarified. "It's not fair to you."

The streets outside become shiny and wet, which makes the

cement look like glass. A green car roars by and splashes water so high that it brings with it a brown leaf, which plasters itself against the window.

"Green cars don't sell, you know," says Joyce, "I also read that in the statistics."

"Really?" Russell takes a swig of his Bud.

"I don't remember where I read that. Some magazine, probably. Something to the effect that for resale, do this and this and such, and the two things I remember from that article are: red cars have more accidents and green cars don't sell."

"Well, I'll have to take that into consideration next time I buy a car," Russell pushes his plate away.

The mood in the restaurant slows and thickens as customers clear and waiters remain in the background, suspended like carrot slices in half-congealed jello. Another aimless day waiting for the haze to clear. The psychic had said, "I see you going down this long dark road… It's almost as if you've lost your way."

Russell has finished his meal and motions for the waitress to bring the check, and once paid up, they head outside and part company at the street entrance to the restaurant, each vowing to keep in touch and not leave the pursuit of friendship up to chance meetings in darkened movie theaters where people often go for quick doses of validation.

She drives in the direction of the setting sun, now near its resting angle in the sky. In the distance, about 500 yards away, she sees the Georgia Dome rising like a sketchy tower of pizza. A large blue billboard sits beside the Dome, and the white lettering on the billboard reads, 'There's Hope In Jesus Christ.'

She parks the car, gets out, stands beside the road, and feels traffic vibrations underfoot. To the left of the Housing and Urban Development building, a street person, a modern-day Thoreau, either unable or unwilling to search his lifetime for the exit door from the mercantile house of horrors, carries a large plastic trash bag half full of aluminum cans. The government building's contribution toward outdoor landscaping, a fountain that sprays water ten feet into the air, mocks as it spews, the sound of leaves blowing in the grass. Her skirt blows fiercely against her knees, yet she feels neither hot nor cold from the wind, only a pleasant, if benign caress.

Behind her, a bronze statue shaped like a woman in a long dress guards the dingy, narrow street where buildings come together in a triangle. The statue holds a bird, a Phoenix rising, whose beak points skyward, upward where clouds churn and rustle together one way today and another way tomorrow.

"But I see you coming to the end of the road," said the psychic, "and there is light all around you. Good things, Joyce. Good things."

THE WIND

"I just wrote a poem in my head," he says as he reclines on his back, one hand caressing her, the other flipping ashes haphazardly into an ashtray.

She rests her knees, drawn up on either side of his ribs into the white chenille bedspread. "Tell me," she whispers the words deliberately into his ear.

Holding steady his head, he recites:

"A circle, our bodies.
Hand to back
Shoulder to knee and thigh,
You and I.
A sign, a symbol closed,
Eternal. Infinite. Forever."

She has been listening too closely lately for that word 'forever.' Has been wanting to know before mortality becomes too comfortable that there is indeed such a word.

"I like it," she raises up and looks at him.

He smiles with a slightly proud twinge, turns to stub out the cigarette, and turns back to speak to her again, "Have I told you lately that I adore you?" He looks at her mouth.

Cold wind blows in through an open window and she reaches down to pull the bedspread over them.

"Listen to that Jaybird raising hell out there," he looks toward the window.

"Why is he fussing?" she asks.

"Jaybirds are always bitching," he says, "they are lazy creatures."

"How do you know?" she asks, truly curious.

"Because they like to come in and take over the food. They steal it and fight for it. They're basically lazy," he says.

She recalls birds gathering around the bird feeder last Spring. The little plastic house had been full of wild birdseed, and a squirrel climbed the tree where the feeder hung, held onto it with nimble feet, and ate most of the seed. Then, still clinging with all fours, the squirrel began to swing with the house until both came crashing down to the ground. The house lay shattered, birdseed lay scattered all over the ground, and the squirrel darted away.

"What kind of bird is the meanest, do you think?" she asks.

"The meanest?" He pronounces the word as if he has never before spoken the word. Not surprising coming from a man who makes it a point to object to labels.

"I would say," he ponders, "probably the vulture."

"Vulture, indeed." She remembers visions of large stark black vultures waiting on fences that line dusty country roads. There is often an abundance of roadkill along dusty backroads to nowhere.

"Yep," he says, "The vulture, scavenger of the desert, the crow, scavenger of the land, the Seagull, scavenger of the water." He speaks loudly over a high wind blowing up outside. It whistles in through cracks in the house, rattles window sills and whips curtains.

"Listen to that wind!" she says. "Do you think we should close the window? Something's blowing up out there."

He looks outside and she asks again, "Do you hear the wind?"

Leaves are blowing like confetti, the trees bending low in sway, "I had better go upstairs and latch the balcony door so it doesn't blow open," he says.

He rises from the bed, swings his legs over to one side and she pushes him forward, her hand resting still on his back. He stands, steps into his pants, pulls on a shirt and walks toward the stairway.

His warmth gone from the bed, she is suddenly cold and shivers beneath the covers. Turning on her side, she draws knees to chest and forms a tight, self-protective hug. Reaching behind her, she feels for the first garment that comes to hand and pulls it toward her. It is her blouse, and she sits under the covers like an Indian under a tent, and proceeds to fully dress.

The fury of the wind has settled long enough to render the room so silent that the only sound present is the steady, almost reverent tick of the clock on the fireplace mantel. Slipping into her loafers, she walks across the soft carpet into a room of the house where she has heretofore only glimpsed in passing: his office. The messy room, he had called it. "We will have to straighten it out one day," he had said.

A long desk holding racks of paper dominates the corner of

the room. Also, sitting beside his computer is several piles of letters and booklets which are flanked by a large ceramic tropical bird on a stand with rubber bands hanging off its nose. The room appears to have a wind source all its own, with a cold draft blowing towards the bookshelves, which causes a shutter to bang against the wall outside.

She walks towards the bookshelf, her eye fixed the entire time on a photograph of him and a woman. Both are beaming into the camera while standing in front of a bright, sunshiny background. She moves closer to the picture, touches the frame and begins to pick it up, but changes her mind, and instead bends down and studies it carefully. His eyes belie a happy expression, his arm circles the woman's shoulders, and in the background palm trees stand dressed in moss. The woman, small and dark, is smiling a somewhat guarded smile - more like a shy grin, and near the bottom of the photo, scrawled almost like an autograph are the words: ALL MY LOVE, RACHEL.

Outside, the wind moans through shrubs as if it has gained a speaking voice, and for a minute she thinks she actually hears words within the sound of the wind. She backs up against the bookshelf, eyes closed, and presses her hands to her breast in an effort to steady and protect herself. Maybe she will push the wind inward.

Feeling the green monster rise from within, she presses harder, forming with spread fingers, a fan-like guard gate across the vulnerable planks of her heart. "I know you," she addresses the chill in the room. "Purposely, I never asked. I never wanted to know," her voice becomes a whisper to the picture.

Still pressed against the shelf, she closes her eyes and inhales for composure, unsure how to steel herself against those who have gone on, yet who still remain. She turns around and looks at the heavy wood claw-footed desk which holds all of his writings. She knows about them, knows of the intended book just before Rachel died.

Now, impulsively, she bounds almost wildly toward the box that holds the papers. His handwriting. Her name. Unashamedly, she begins to read:

Rachel and I are very much in love. She is happy, she feels safe despite the diagnosis. She stops reading and shuts her eyes tight in an effort to forget what she has seen. Her heart pounds like a bird trying to free itself, yet she picks up another paper and reads, It is the voice. It always starts with the voice, the beautiful… "No!" she flings the papers to the floor.

"No, I can't! Why am I doing this?!"

He appears at the door, startled, and speaks quickly, "What's going on here?"

She jerks her head back and looks at him through savage eyes while he stands looking at the papers strewn on the floor like so many flapjacks on a conveyor belt. He opens his mouth to speak, but only searches her face with bewilderment. For a long moment the only sound is the rattle of an aging casement window, and a tinkle of glass outside as the wind continues to rage.

Slowly he walks towards her holding out his hands, palms toward the floor, "The wind is coming up strong," he says.

"Yes," she begins to shake her head as tears grow insistent, "It is."

"It's going to be another rough day at sea," he comes closer, but very gradually, like molasses.

"Not a good day for sailing, Mate?" she wipes her eyes with the back of her hand.
"No, love, not a good day," he reaches her now, and very gently presses one shoulder and then the other toward him while he wraps both arms behind her back, holding her captive and certain.

"What?" he whispers into her hair.

"Nothing," she lies.

"Ask me," he presses.

"No," she answers, "I don't want to know. I never wanted to know."

"Yeah?" he attempts to raise her face to his gaze level, thumb under her chin, to look into her eyes, see into her torture.

"I still don't. I'm not ready," she holds her head down purposely averting her foolish eyes.

He says nothing, but still in the lingering embrace, they begin to sway very slightly back and forth almost like a mother would rock her baby or a father would soothe his child.

"What I have with you," he begins, "I have never had with anyone."

"Yes," she says, "And what you had with her, you don't have with me."

He poses no argument; he knows she knows him too well. He will not, with her, purposely cloud his words. "Tell me," he raises her chin again, impatient now, "How can I ease your pain?"

"You can't," she glares into his eyes, sees the flicker of white with powder blue, "My pain will always be with me. I come to you this way."

"I wish I had met you when I was sixteen," he frowns to punctuate, "I wish a lot of things. Things could have been so different."

She wants to throw it out. Some word. Some smart retort. Some device to make him see the contradiction of his thoughts.

"If that were so, you would have missed out on the person who meant the most to you in life. Her!" She points to the helpless picture, the deceased spouse, innocent in its stance there on the bookshelf.

In frustration, he pulls his hands away, brings them close to his face and studies them as if he were trying to read his very own palms, "How long have we known one another?" he asks.

But the question goes unanswered, and she begins to tremble again. "Just promise me," she begins, "that when the day arrives that I become as important to you as she was, that you will tell me."

He opens his mouth to speak, but no words come out. He brushes his hands across his eyes, lowers his head, and begins to nod ever so slightly as if to say 'okay,' then he looks back at her. "You know," he smiles brightly, "Sometimes you remind me of a little girl who needs a good spanking. Is that what you want?"

This is a game they play often, but it angers her now. How could he be so callous, sweep it under the run so easily? She lets all the air out of her lungs in one quick swoosh and turns to walk out of the room, brushing past him in a huff.

"Wait a minute," he says, "Come back here. I don't understand. What is wrong?" He reaches a hand toward her as she passes him, "Beth, everyone is insecure! Some more so than others. I can...."

But, she is gone from the room, and is in the living room hastily pulling on her coat. He rushes to her, places both hands on her shoulders and whirls her around to face him, "I said," he insists, "What is wrong?"

Very calmly she surveys every feature about his face. The powder-blue eyes, the high cheekbones and long English jaw, the mustache that hides a nice and sometimes crooked smile, the level gaze which belies wisdom beyond his years. Almost mutely, she responds, "Anger is a wind that blows out the light of the mind."

"Listen," his fingers tighten on her shoulders, "There is something in you that is trying to destroy what we have because you don't think you deserve to be happy." He looks hard into her eyes, "Don't listen to it!"

She pulls away and walks toward the front door. He stands dazed, his arms now hanging straight down by his side, his head cocked, posed and puzzled. "I think..." he begins to slowly follow her toward the door.

She flings open the door and it, buoyed by the fiercely blowing wind, slaps meanly against the house. "I think you are being unfair," he calls into the wind at her back, "I love you!"

The wind takes his words and jumbles them with the trees and with the birdseed scattered on the ground as leaves begin to dive after her and swirl around her like embittered vultures. She stumbles in the driveway on round acorns the squirrels should have hidden away ages ago. One last time, the wind catches her hair, digs it into her eyes, all the while blowing lights out of her heart like fragile little birthday candles on a tiny little pink cake.

BEYOND GODOT

I came home weary from the party, leaned over to take off my blouse, and smelled Bob. I haven't seen him in ages, so this must be a blouse I hung up without washing. Thinking back, I remember when last I wore it. We had made love, half-clothed, caught in a rush, our fully clothed chests pressed against one another while he whispered, "I love you so much I want to cry. Will you remember that?" he had asked, and I had said, "Yes, I will. I will remember."

At the party, I sat twirling my wine, looking for friends, none to whom I could come right out and say, 'I want to run away forever with a man named Bob. I want to spend my life, you see, talking to him and sharing a half liter of Chianti with him in some dark, cheap Italian restaurant where no one ever goes.'

I began the evening wearing my newfound confidence like an unsoiled garment. Nancy, some producer for CNN, was there. At first, I felt on her level, esteem-wise. She was loud, very sure of herself, and as I watched her talking, her mouth thrown open wide when she laughed, I could see not a single cavity in her head. That really intimidated me! I thought everyone had cavities. Perhaps her cavities were filled with white fillings, I don't know. Maybe she was simply, as everyone seems (except me), perfect. I kept thinking that Bob would probably have liked her because he likes aggressive women. Once, he actually said so.

Sitting here feeling jealous of her confident advantages, I watched Nancy further sparkle as she talked to her boyfriend, some guy who is rumored to have dated Julia Roberts, and I thought: Bob would definitely find her sexy. I'm glad he isn't here.

Dave, the host of the party, walked over to me and sat down. He leaned closely, touching my shoulder with his and asked, "How are things with you?"

"Oh, great," I answered, "Just great!" But, had he looked closely, he would have seen that my eyes were saying, "I have taken leave of my senses, Dave. I am in love and there is no good reason for it."

"How's the acting going?" he asked.

"It is good," I said, "I am going to get lucky this year. I feel it!"

And then I found myself telling him how I had finally broken away from the homesickness of Oklahoma. I told him I had bought my son a guitar for his birthday, and I told him Neil, my ex-husband, was making money hand over fist, that he and Linda would probably get entirely out of debt by Christmas.

"That is marvelous!" Dave said.

Money is always marvelous, I thought, as I sipped my wine. I set the wine glass back on the coffee table in front of me, and, flirting with the idea that I would not stay long, I aligned its rim evenly over the coaster as I sat planning an early departure.

Dave's apartment looked very nice for the party. Clearly, he had gone to some trouble. He had bunched candles in three different places on the table, and the place flickered with a warm, almost pinkish glow. Also, there was one more bunch of about nine short candles burning at the kitchen bar behind me. There was another assortment of six or seven, all different sizes of candles, that sat on top of one of the stereo speakers. All the others graced the dining room table, glowing over an inviting and aesthetically pleasing array of food. Of course, Dave's Partner, Fredrick, had done all of the work putting the party together.

Fredrick was the artistic one of the duo, while Dave was the money-maker, the provider, the take-charge guy who alternately expressed his love for Fredrick in one breath and woefully agonized over Fredrick's drinking and his own codependence in the other.

I considered getting up to pour myself a cup of coffee because I like the looks of coffee floating in pretty china cups, and they had some dynamite-looking china on display on the table! But, before I could get up, Nancy scooted over to sit in the chair beside me. She crossed her long legs, boot-clad halfway up to her knees, she interlaced her fingers over her flat tummy, and addressed me, "So, what do you do?"

I liked her. I really did. But I hate to answer questions about what I do because that always leads to the fact that I don't do anything, and from there, the interview usually graduates to the revelation that I have a child, and then I typically get asked how old he is. Of course, everyone is pretty proficient in simple math. By the time the inquisitor hears his age, the interrogation ends with, "My God, you don't look old enough to have a 22-year-old son. You don't look much older than 22 yourself!"

I think the only reason I look young for my age is that I never grew much past 5'2", almost as if people are still waiting for me to have my growing spurt. I can't figure it out. I keep thinking someday my body will catch up with myself, but so far it hasn't happened. Well, I usually lie about my age because I never think about age. Not really. There are a million more pressing things to think about than age.

I picked up my wine glass to keep my hands occupied and not flail as I talked. That is another bad habit of mine, possibly a genetic Italian gesture I could not get rid of if I wanted to. I think I am merely self-conscious and find it challenging to look into people's eyes, so I wave my hands when I talk to distract people. Ordinarily, I wouldn't notice I do this except people generally end up watching my hands when I speak as if I might be trying to hypnotize them rather than converse with them. Nothing could be further from the truth. I'm just trying like everybody to get by in this world, and that's a fact!

"I mean," Nancy addressed me again, "Where do you work?"

"Well," I said, "I'm an actress, so I guess I don't really work."

"No joke?" she smiled, her eyes widening as she appeared to forget that I had just said I do nothing. "What have you done? Have I seen you?" she asked.

"Maybe," I said, "I just finished a pizza commercial. Did you see that by any chance?"

"Oh, tell me about it! I don't know! Maybe." She seemed pretty excited. She uncrossed her legs and sat up straighter in the chair, and began to wave her own hands around. "Which one?"

I placed my glass back on the table and immediately felt new energy. "It goes like this," I began. "I enter the pizza place with the guy who plays my husband. Also, the kid who plays my kid... see, in the commercial, I play a mommie."

"A mommie. I love it!" she scooted around in the chair.

"Yeah, I play a mom, and there is this pizza contest going on, and I toss my husband the car keys... because I think in the contest you win a car or something... anyway, and I say, 'Go for it, honey!' meaning the car."

"Oh, that's great!" She said, "Do it again."

I focused straight ahead, staring at Dave's curtains that covered the sliding glass door as if they were a camera lens, turned my face slightly to the left because my right side is my good side, and I said, smiling the way I did in the commercial, "Go for it, honey!"

"Wow! Charles," she reached across the room toward the guy she came with, "Come here! She did a pizza commercial. Have you seen it? Does she look familiar to you?"

Charles looked at me as he walked across the room, narrowing his eyes, "Uh-huh," he said, "Kinda."

Charles had that young, lean face with high cheekbones, little ears, and curly hair. He was probably an actor himself. He had the kind of young, sexy look I used to adore until I met Bob. I'll be honest: another reason I was sensitive about my age was because I used to like younger guys. Kept getting crushes on my leading men.

"So, what else have you done?" Nancy was now facing Charlie, who was standing beside her chair, "Do you do any stage?"

"Oh, heavens yes," I said, "If I didn't do stage, I would feel like I wasn't working. Film parts are few and far between."

In the background, I thought I heard rumba music starting up from somewhere, and that seemed oddly appropriate. The beat began a restless stir in me that found me considering leaving the party so I could be by the phone in case Bob decided to call from the film set in lower Africa. It would be morning by now in Africa.

Bob was a wonderful actor, better than I was, actually. Which, when I thought about it, is probably why he was on a film set in lower Africa and I was at a wine and cheese birthday party at Dave and Fredrick's. Besides, there is a demand for 50-year-old male actors who can still memorize lines. It's surprising how many actors have fried out by 50.

Before Bob got this lucrative film part, he had been cast in the touring company of Shakespeare on the Lawn, a professional group based in Louisville. But, a week into rehearsals, the company went bust from a combination of dwindling corporate donations and over-expenditures by the Shakespeare Company. Just like that, one day Bob was back 'pounding the pavement' (or in the acting business, 'out of work').

Nancy had picked up a carrot stick from the tempting display at the dining table, which dangled a dot of dip on the end just before she took a bite, "Now I think I know where I've seen you," she pointed the remainder of the carrot stick at me.

Funny how luck runs. Right before the Shakespeare job fell through for Bob, he also lost his job at the furniture store. In a panic, he called an old corporate friend and asked for a real job. The friend had said, "Maybe. Let's discuss it over lunch."

"Where did you see me?" I asked Nancy, looking at the carrot stick still pointed at me.

"Did you play Gertie in the musical OKLAHOMA?" She popped the rest of the carrot in her mouth and chewed with her even, cavity-free, white teeth.

"I most certainly did," I said. "You saw that?"

"Oh, you were wonderful," she tossed her hair and slipped an arm around her boyfriend, who was now sitting on the arm of the chair next to her.

"Thank you," I said in true humility because it always surprises me when a fan comes forth. They turn up in the most unlikely of places.

Dave strolled over and placed his arm softly on my shoulder as he addressed Nancy, "Jena is a wonderful actress," his speech betraying traces of a proper Southern upbringing from a man who was equally gracious on the inside.

"Well, you both are very kind," I said.

"No, it's true," Dave insisted.

"So, how can you say you do nothing?" asked Nancy, in a feisty, almost challenging manner.

"I don't know," I looked at my feet and aligned my toes, positioning one slightly behind the other.

"Give yourself credit, girl," she continued. "In my job at CNN, I see actors all the time, and all their stories of their struggles are interesting, but different."

I felt alone and on display without Bob by my side to help deflect attention. Would the success of the film job change him? I remembered the day we had waited in the busy restaurant for his Corporate friend, who seemed to hold the lifeline to the real world, a world that both beckons the hungry artist, yet repels him at the same time. We had sat there that day half-broke, hoping Mr. Jenkins would spring for lunch. But time passed, and he didn't show anyway. We had watched as business-suited men and women filed past, their pre-ordained importance perched on their shoulders or directly ahead of them: men who had arrived in starched white shirts and wearing round glasses. Women who had varied only minutely, wearing virtually the same uniform: navy blue monotony with shoulder bags not too bulky. Bob and I had remained patiently above it or beneath it, indeed not of it.

"Bob," I had begged him that day, "Don't take a 9-to-5!"

"Just for a short time," he had leaned his head against the booth as we had continued to watch the door for a man who was either too busy, too rude, or too important to keep a luncheon date with a couple of deadbeat, out-of-work actors who probably only wanted a job out of him anyway.

"It'll only be temporary. I promise," he had cupped my chin and traced one finger along my cheek. "It's just a way," he had continued, "to get from point A to point B."

The Hostess had walked over to us and had asked, "Have you been… do we have your name on the wait list?"

"Yes," Bob had said, "but we are waiting on someone."

Even then, it had struck me funny, as we sat there with enough money between us to buy an order of fries, how, although everyone else filed in and out of the restaurant with an obvious purpose in life, they seemed to me to be extras in a movie, and we, the stars, were merely waiting. Waiting for Godot. I had laughed at the thought.

"What's so funny?" Bob had asked, his own face giving way to a grin because he never could exactly figure me out.

"I feel like we are in a movie," I had said, "here we sit, waiting like a couple of ninnies, like those two idiots who were waiting for Godot. He never came, you know."

"Who, Godot?" Bob still grinned.

"Yeah, Godot never came. That was the point of the play, wasn't it?" I had asked.

"On the contrary," Bob had answered, "he came for each one of those people. Godot was to each one of those people whatever they believed him to be."

"These people," I had pointed to the crowd filing by us, "seem to have deadlines. We don't. We're idle - waiting on someone. We're waiting for Godot!"

"We are, no doubt, beyond Godot," Bob had said. "Let's go,"

he had said, his tone of voice a level of calm I found almost scary.

After that day of the aborted luncheon, Bob finally got that acting break. His Agent called and signed him to play a renegade pioneer in the depths of the jungle. He was to portray a man relentless in his search for truth, a man who would not be put off by facts, figures, or reality - no small stretch for Bob.

"One girl," Nancy had now dipped several pieces of vegetables in dip and had placed them on a paper plate which she held on her knees, "one girl that I interviewed is famous, yet all she wants is to be happily married and drive a Station Wagon full of kids and dogs."

I watched her hold a cucumber in one hand, which had been reduced from a perfect circle to a crescent by just one bite, a bit of dip dotting the corner of her mouth.

"That seems so easy to me," I said. "How difficult is it? I mean, can't anyone, just anyone, drive a station wagon and load it up with kids and dogs?"

"You'd be surprised," she said.

Fredrick walked over to me for the first time during the evening. He wore a black taffeta jacket over a white ruffled shirt, and at his neck and down the front of the shirt dangled a sparkling tie made of nothing but rhinestones. On one hand, he wore a Liberace-sized conglomeration of stones on one finger, and on the other hand, he wore one tastefully cut and sized single gem.

"Darl-i-n-g," he announced as if I had just walked into the party, "It is so lovely to see you, as ever."

"Thank you," I reached up one arm to hug him. This was a thing between us, these hugs.

"Oh, you look divine," his inflection trailed upward at the end.

"Thank you very much. And, so do you," I said.

Fredrick was tall, thin, with black hair, black eyes, and a very dignified-looking aquiline nose. He claimed to be a descendant of Spanish royalty, and there was some rumor that he was from a family of famous Hollywood has-beens who were temporarily down on their luck. I had never pressed Fredrick for history because I loved the presence he presented better than any precursor he could relate or fabricate.

"I feel so delicious," he began to touch his face. "I had my hair done. I had a facial. I had my nails done." He held his hands out in front of him, and began to study first his shiny fingertips, then his pieces of jewelry. Placing his thumb behind his ring finger on his right hand, he massaged to a forward position the large single-stone ring, which had slipped because of the sheer weight of the stone, around to the back of his hand. "Did you see this?" he asked.

"Couldn't miss it," I said. "I love it. It's beautiful," I said, knowing full well that in some cases the authenticity of an object is much less momentous than its effect. Could an actress claim otherwise?

Fredrick leaned down and kissed my hair, "Your hair smells

lovely, my dear."

"Thank you," I reached up and guided his cheek as he straightened, and then he patted my back as he turned back into the crowd.

Nancy had cut herself a piece of chocolate cake and had carried it into the room in her right hand, holding a china cup of coffee in her left. "Can I get anyone some cake while I'm up?" she addressed the room.

"Here, let me," Dave came from across the room and centered him- self at the table, "Who would like what? I'm officially taking food orders."

I stood to excuse myself, I picked up my evening clutch, intending to duck into the powder room. I had been here to Dave and Fredrick's house many times before, so I knew my way around, and since no one seemed to notice that I was about to leave the room, I pondered for a few moments that maybe I might just slip out the front door instead. On impulse, I turned on my heel and began walking toward the front door. Most of the party had adjourned to the dining table, standing facing the giant chocolate cake that had now been scored into several pieces. Oddly, the front door seemed further away from me now than it had seemed earlier in the evening, as if the room might have grown in size to accommodate a larger-than-life situation happening in my own head. But I desperately needed fresh air. Maybe I could simply cut short my jaunt through the front room and slip out the patio door, but I also knew there were animals out on the patio. There was Dancer, a large dog who most of the time lived in the spare bedroom, but who was shuffled outside in the event of parties.

Glancing once more into the kitchen, I could see steam and smoke rise from hot water and candles. A white ceiling fan breezed lazily over the cooktop isle, flickering the candles that sat on the bar, which had now burned low, some of them dripping white wax onto the countertop.

The front door stood slightly ajar as if someone else had slipped outside, and not wishing to completely ostracize themselves from the festivities within, had pulled it only scantily to, so I quickly slipped out the half-open door.

Outside, the porch was dark with only tiny stars peppering the night sky like rhinestones on black velvet. I heard a stirring and saw to the right of me, leaning off the deck of the patio, Nancy's date, Charles. He stood, flicking reddened ashes from his cigarette onto holly bushes below.

My first instinct was to look the other way and pretend that I had not seen him, to begin walking up the street as if to walk to my car, but what would I do once I reached the car? Yell back like the phony actress that I am and say: Hey, Charles. Didn't see you there. Well, good meeting you..and I really liked Nancy. Well, nice seeing you, and take care. Tippecanoe and Tyler, too.

Instead, I relented and began to walk toward the direction of the deck. Charles stood, his profile an opaque silhouette against a sheer, dry breath of an evening. He stood like Heathcliff on the moor, waiting. I walked, Heather in the sky, waiting. Waiting we were, each of us waiting for whatever it was we wanted it to be. I knew even before I reached the deck where he was standing and stepped onto the first wooden rung leading upward to where he was that everywhere, everyone was waiting.

THE NEXT CENTURY

Annie stands in front of the mirror and ties a black scarf over her ears. To shield the sun off her face, she dons a wide-brimmed, green felt hat trimmed with tan, braided leather and a feather. It is February, but the air is unseasonably warm. Squirrels run up and down trees and birds hop around like it was an early spring day. She buttons her brown coat all the way up to the neck, and pulls on matching brown gloves, then throws on one final scarf around her neck. The walk to the library is a 20-minute walk, and the wind will be chilly despite the sun.

Dressed this way she looks a bit odd and she knows it. The hat, once considered high fashion, is crushed and worn now. These days she is more familiar with poverty than with keeping up with the Joneses, and she has joint pains and survival tactics paramount on her mind.

She walks down a narrow pebble walkway which is overgrown with bush that turned to briars when all the leaves fell off. She puts both hands in front of her eyes to shield the twigs from hitting her as she walks through them. Once outside the brushy area and near the street, she startles the driver of a white Chevrolet by her sudden emergence, and he swerves as if he is afraid she might break out a tire tool and turn it on him.

Playful child sounds ring in a distance with shrills of tag or hide-and-seek, and the roar of big wheel tricycles can be heard on the city sidewalks. A small void in her remembers Richard when they were still together, the magic in the least things like spring days or falling leaves. She feels it through a numb veil, which serves to render his past presence unreal the same way a dream slips away to become nonsense by noon. Nevertheless, she remembers the squareness of his jaw, his high ears, the straight line of hair trimmed against a pale neck. Sometimes his nearness is so real she sways, undecided which to believe, the memory or the moment.

Before her, the squares of the sidewalk stretch out. Newly poured, each square looks perfectly equal. After a patch of new cement, she comes again upon the old cement, cracked and crumbly. A tree root grows out of one old patch, its roots lifting the cement square of the ground almost six inches out of alignment with the others. Beside the tree trunk, one bunch of yellow crocus peeks up like little scoops of butter on green straws.

She walks by a large three-story house with a screened-in garden room that has become a catch-all junk room for lamps and tables by people who desperately need either a storage room or a garage sale. She turns right at the corner and proceeds down a commercial strip of land where she passes a mannequin that stands in the window of a dress shop wearing the same dress it has worn for two weeks now. Closer to the window, she peers in through hands cupped against the glaring sun. A large dog sits in the window beside the mannequin and with the movement, raises his head to look at her, the black fur around its mouth arranged like a smile. She smiles back, taps the window a couple of times, shifts her shoulder bag to the other shoulder, and walks on. Two men walk ahead.

"Well, he had that Bulimia. Ya know whar they're not eatin'. They said he was on a watermelon diet," one man said.

"Yeah," said the other man.

"I like watermelon and all, but not that much!" said the other.

"He really did have some uniforms. Didn't he? He'd come out in that one rhinestone cape when he was playin' in Vegas that weighed, I ferget how much they said..." he continued.

"Now, that there's probably what got him down - wearin' round all them costumes."

"Oh, yeah."

Traffic whizzes past so fast it misses the day. It wheels by the aborted tile, the tiny crocus, the rock houses sitting up on steep lots. It whirls to wherever traffic goes in it's mania, breaking the limit of speed and tearing into the next century as if it has nothing in common with this one.

She passes the men and proceeds down a block of businesses on 51st, rumored to be Mafia-owned, where a black 3-door limo with darkened windows sits like a long sleek lizard. An immaculately groomed and suited man, carrying a burgundy briefcase walks out of a bar, crosses the street, and heads for the grocery store parking lot. Once, on a walk with Richard down this same street, she wore a different hat and he had commented, "Annie," he had said, "have you noticed how everyone is staring at you in that hat?"

But, it had been summer then and the hat served more to shield the sun than to keep her warm. That day, she had been wearing a black sundress and a black Liz Claiborne hat with a black veil. Her long red hair hung down past her shoulders beneath the hat, and she looked as if she might be just returning from a funeral.

"Why, do I look funny?" she had asked.

"I think you look beautiful," he had answered.

"Do you think I've changed?" she had fished for a clue to his distant behavior.

He had squinted into the sun, "You talk faster," he had said.

"I was so afraid you'd find me changed."

But he was the one who had changed. They had walked that day up a hill and into a music store because he was getting hot and had begun to ask if she knew where there was an 'inside' shopping center bar where he could get a beer.

After cooling off in the music store, they had pressed on toward a fountain where they sat to rest and where they had sprinkled water on each other. "Let me take your picture in front of it," Richard had said.

In the picture, she sits smiling shyly into the camera with sun in the background as bright as a butterscotch halo. Golden highlights dance off her hair hanging long beneath the hat, and her skin looks a pale ivory against the black sundress that has ties at the shoulders. The picture is in her album as dead and old now as the memory.

She walks into the library and lays her heavy bag on a long wooden table. She removes the green felt hat, unties the black scarf, removes the gloves, the coat, and other scarf. Neatly, she folds the scarves and places them with gloves inside her bag.

The library is buzzing with an energy of silenced excitement. People sit all around, many at tables by themselves. In the corner along a wall that is nothing but windows, a bearded man dozes on a couch, half-strutted out, his sack of possessions resting beneath his feet like a makeshift ottoman. One very obese man reads the New York Times, holding the paper so close to his nose, reading with eyes cast up over glasses that rest low on his nose. The expression raises his eyebrows and creates wrinkles in four rows along the width of his forehead.

Annie walks toward the windowed wall and passes wire racks holding yellow, blue, and other colored pamphlets telling of various meeting places for Past Life Readings and Channeling events. Standing at the wall, she presses her forehead against the glass and realizes that the library is very hot. The glass feels cool thanks to outside air. She looks out the window downward and sees for the pleasure of the library viewing audience, that below lies a well-maintained rock and cactus garden. A fountain spills into a fake rock bed on one side of the garden and driftwood mixed with quartz crystal lies all around like plastic polka dots. At least, she thinks it is quartz. Once in an Earth Science class at college the subject of rocks was discussed. All kinds of different rocks were passed around in class after the professor gave a droning explanation of each one: where it was found, how it was formed, whether it would or would not leave a colored mark when scratched on limestone. At the time, making an "A" seemed more important than remembering anything about rocks. She decides the funniest line in the play Vanities is when the character Joanne says, 'I want to go to college, but I sure don't care to learn anything.'

Looking upward from the garden, she sees the clear sky and the shining sun. The day makes her feel new energy and like not wanting to be in the library after all. She fishes in her purse for a quarter, disappears around the corner, drops the quarter into a pay phone slot and dials.

There are two rings and Dean answers on the third ring, "Property Management Services."

"Dean," she says brightly into the phone.

"Annie," he says, "What's up?"

"It is such a beautiful day," she begins.

"Tell me about it," he nearly groans.

"Actually, it started out fairly chilly," she says.

"It IS February, you know," he says.

"Yes, but it is nearly spring," she says.

"Uh, not quite," he says, "what's on your mind? Surely you didn't call me up to discuss the weather."

"The sun has been shining since early morning," she ignores his question.

"I wouldn't know," he retorts, "I've been working 7:00 to 3:00 flex-time lately, and sun is barely awake at that hour. Very much like everyone else around here."

"Oh, come on, Dean, you work for the government. What do you expect?" she laughs, "How many years has it been since you've seen anyone alive, for that matter?"

"Very funny," he says. "Okay, you call me up to insult me or what?"

"No, actually, I was wondering," she begins.

"Yes," he says.

"Why don't we have lunch?" she says.

"That sounds good," he says, a relieved tone to his voice.

"Let's have a long lunch," she continues, "like take an extra hour or something."

"I could go for that," he says, "I've got time coming."

"You always seem to have time on your hands," she says, "I'm jealous. Sometimes."

"So, where did you have in mind?" he asks.

"I want to ride around in your convertible," she says, "top down, of course."

"In February?" he exclaims.

"It's a beautiful day, believe me. I walked to the library all bundled up, and then I realized when I got here that I was burning up," she pokes at her coat as she says this.

"Well, for one thing, you might just have worked up some heat through sheer exercise, dummy," he says. "Besides, you might be coming down with something. Ever think about that?"

"No, couldn't be," she says, "I feel too energetic for that."

"Well, that's good to hear," he says. "I don't want to catch something."

"So," she pauses and waits. "See you soon, then?"

"Yeah, sure, high noon," he says. "See you at 12:00 or thereabout." "Okay. Pick me up here at the library," she says bye, and hangs up the phone.

She reaches into her coat pocket for her scarf which she will tie around her head when she rides in Dean's convertible in the open air like Lana Turner did in Body and Soul.

As she gathers her things, she decides to double-check to see if Andrew Greeley's newest book is out, however, as she steps out of the telephone alcove, an elderly lady, who has been waiting, gives her a glare.

Annie has been working very diligently lately to erect boundaries and resist the need to constantly apologize for her space, so she glares back at the lady in a defiance to succumb to any feelings of undeserved guilt. She brushes past the sour-looking woman, then immediately feels shame by sheer advantage of youth and health. But, no, she thinks, no guilt. No bad feelings today of any kind!

The temperature in the library seems to have become even more warm, so she decides to wait by the large glass door and watch for Dean where she can at least watch trees bristle blossom buds high up the limb. Stuffing everything she can into her bag, she ties on the second scarf, dons sunglasses, and dismisses the idea of checking on the status of any new books today.

Shortly, Dean whirls into the parking lot in his new red convertible, sees her immediately, and waves as if she might not have seen him.

She pushes through the doors, walks to the passenger side and flings her stuff in the back floorboard without opening the door. He has the top down and all the windows are down, so the car sits there as accessible as if it has been sawed in half.

She opens the door, slides in the seat and resists the temptation to fasten her seat belt.

"Oh, no," Dean says harshly, "Fasten your seat belt!"

Annie, a late bloomer who has only recently come to resent any tone that passes for one of authority, stares at him open-mouthed, "What good are seat belts in a convertible, you tell me!"

"It's the law," he says, "Buckle up!"

"Yes, but it doesn't make a lot of sense," she mumbles as she reluctantly fastens the seatbelt.

The sun is directly overhead and it glares down on them. But, to her it feels nice and warm, a fine balance to the coolness that now swirls in and encircles the open vehicle once it is going faster.

"Dean," she leans her head back against the headrest, "let's drive over the toll bridge and look at the water."

He says nothing, but turns the car toward the right, away from the Plaza and towards the toll bridge that reminds her, for all in the world, though she has never seen it, what the Golden Gate Bridge might look like.

"Annie," he says as a friend who knows her well, "when are you going to wake up and quit pretending?"

She feels a jolt from his words, "What do you mean pretending?"

"You know exactly what I mean," he says, "pretending you are living a productive life, pretending you are around the corner from greatness, pretending Richard is around the corner somewhere, waiting."

"I don't call it pretending," she says. She bites the tip of her fingernail, "Ever hear of positive thinking? or visualization?"

"Yup," he pops his lips together, "I don't think it's the same thing."

"Well, I do," she says and scoots back in the seat and rolls her head away so she can watch out the car at the trees streaming past them, most of them as barren as if a giant vacuum just swept through town.

"And, today," he continued, "This isn't a warm day. Damn, I'm freezing my ass off!"

"Would it help," she asks gently, "if we roll up the windows?"

He nods yes, but drives on staring straight ahead, making no move to hit the power control buttons which will whip all four windows up as fast as a raindrop can turn into a freezing pellet of ice.

"I don't mean to sound harsh," he says as he carefully watches the road ahead, "I really don't."

"I know you don't," she says while she surveys through the passenger seat side view mirror a man in a pickup truck behind them. He wears a flannel shirt and she can see peeking above his collar a white band that looks like those that rim insulated underwear.

"Go ahead, Dean," she says, "roll up the windows. I don't mind. It will still be fun just having the top down, being able to see up. I like the feeling of having nothing above me. The idea of having all that space up there that stretches out…who knows how far."

Dean glances at her while he carefully pushes the buttons that make each window steadily rise to become a thin if not transparent buffer against the breeze.

"Besides," she says, "you're right. I might be coming down with something."

"You think so?" he looks genuinely concerned. "It's going around at work," he continues, "the flu. It's pretty bad. Some people have been off work almost two weeks."

She laughs, throws her head back and issues forth a throaty sound that Liz Taylor used once when she talked to gossip columnists about Richard Burton, "You guys down at the good old Government get all that sick leave. What else have you got to do but use it?"

"And, what is this all of a sudden about government workers? When, Annie, did you become so," he searches for the perfect word, "militant?"

"Militant!" She laughs into the wind, "How could you use that word to describe me?" She removes her sunglasses and tosses them onto the floorboard. Fiercely, she leans against the dash and allows a sob to usher upward from her heart until she shakes about the shoulders and wets both hands with tears held so deep and long that she wonders where they had been hiding.

"Annie," Dean steers the car towards the side of the road where he gradually comes to a stop.

She feels every movement of the car much more clearly with eyes closed, much the same way blind people often compensate for their handicap with increased awareness in other areas.

"Annie," Dean cups her shoulder with his hand, "come here." He pulls her close, pushes her face into the curve of his neck and she smells the tang of lemon-lime aftershave.

"You know I don't mean to hurt your feelings," he continues. "I just… something's got to wake you up, Sleeping Beauty, before it's too late. I worry because I can see you aren't doing well."

She stiffens in protest, but changes her mind and allows her head to rest on his shoulder while a flood of tears flows like fallen leaves floating down creek water in a stream beside an old farmhouse.

"I think," he says, "I believe you need to get a job. I think you have too much time on your hands."

She dries lingering tears on her shirt sleeve and extends her feet into the floorboard to push herself more straight into the car seat. He raises her chin and looks her sternly in the eyes, "Do you realize what a luxury it is to be able to simply call up someone and say, 'Let's go have lunch' or 'I want to ride around in your convertible!"

"So," she says, knowing full well that she is acting like a spoiled child.

"That's a good example of what I am talking about!" He almost shoves her hands back at her.

Suddenly, she is stunned into silence. She looks through the foggy windshield and sees the beloved toll bridge far in the distance sitting in this February mist like a vision in a dream.

"And, this bit about driving over to that freakin' toll bridge!," he shouts, "How many people, do you think, I let talk me into getting into my car, top down, driving god-knows-how-many miles just to pay for the privilege of driving over a toll bridge! Some god-forsaken toll bridge!"

She wants to say something completely inappropriate like 'please don't curse,' or 'don't take the Lord's name in vain,' but she allows the words to freeze in her mouth much like the sobbing that eventually froze in her heart months ago.

"Annie, precious," his voice is gentle as once again he leans toward her, "your love affair is over."

Once when she was a child, she had a remembrance of descending a wide staircase in a large house in her pajamas. From her upstairs bedroom, she had been awakened by loud music and laughter on the back lawn. Rising from her slumber, she had proceeded slowly down the staircase trailing her hand behind her along the bannister. At the bottom of the stairs she looked to the left and saw that beyond the French doors, which had been opened onto the warm night, a garden party was in progress. She saw beautifully dressed women in flowing dresses and handsomely dressed men in black suits and shiny shoes. At the bottom of the stairs she noticed that there were empty glasses littering every table and surface in the dining and living room area. She walked over to one of the glasses, picked it up and smelled it, and it smelled like a fine bourbon.

Whereas the house had prevailed in her mind as her paramount defining childhood experience, her mother told her that she must have dreamed that because they had never lived in a two-story house. Ever.

Dean reaches over and unties her scarf. He pulls off the scarf and folds it into a square about the size of a wallet. With his right hand, he reaches out and pushes strands of hair out of her eyes. "You have beautiful eyes, Annie," he says.

"Thank you," she says. "In high school we had a contest where we voted on 'best' things. I was voted as having the most beautiful eyes."

Dean frowns and looks out the window, "That's an unusual thing to vote on."

"I think so too," she says.

She hears a thin mechanical sound and sees through the rear-view mirror that Dean is slowly raising the top, its automated action being controlled as nearly everything else on the car, by an electrical button located in some safe and strategic location.

"Annie," he says, "I'll do almost anything you ask. But, I will not waste any more time driving over to some broken-down toll bridge, and I will not be responsible for you catching Pneumonia."

"I just wish Spring would come," she whispers as she studies his face. Is he angry? He has a kind face, almost too serious, though. She looks at his ear lobes to see if he has those diagonal creases which are supposed to indicate a tendency to massive heart failure at some point. His ears are not creased, or maybe he is too young for that kind of thing to show up.

He gets out of the car and clamps the top down on his side, then he walks around to her side, opens the door, leans against the top, and, pushing it into position, he clamps it closed. Holding the door open with his knee, he squats beside her there on the shoulder of the road where traffic roars, passing them going ninety miles an hour. "You know," he says, "I would kiss you if it would help."

"It probably wouldn't," she says.

"I know," he says, and gently he leans in to place a warm, full kiss on her mouth. It feels better than she ever thought it would.

He rises, dusts off his pant leg, shuts the door and walks back to his side of the car. He stands there a short second as he waits for cars to pass, choosing not to open the door in the path of such oncoming ferocity.

Once in the car, he turns down the heater to a lower level, pulls away from the shoulder of the road, and swings a large "U" in the middle of the freeway.

Driving back in the opposite direction, the car is silent except for the soft purr of the heater. Annie visualizes that upon each passing telephone pole there hangs a sign that reads:

WELCOME BACK ANNIE. WELCOME BACK HOME.

NIGHT MUSIC

I once said to Mike, "I believe that waves wash us in the direction that we are meant to go." He frowned, as he often did, but I continued, "Because sitting here today with you - that is something I never would have planned."

His frown graduated to a scowl, "Not true," he said. "Choices! Our lives are nothing more than the sum of our choices!"

Although this early conversation should have been a clue, I was to learn in many ways how opposite Mike and I really were. Opposites attract, they say, but how do they fare over the long haul?

Mike intrigued me. In many ways, he resembled a vampire even though he didn't actually stay up all night, and he obviously didn't drink blood. It's just that he never had what I could call a 'complete history.' His dad had died, he said. His mother lived somewhere in the Carolinas. He had once worked at a summer resort with a girl who wanted to commit suicide, yet they ended up having a summer romance.

He had a way about him, however. He captured my interest without much effort on his part because he wasn't particularly thoughtful or romantic. As long as I knew him, I never knew him to follow through on anything.

He had written a play which was being produced in Kansas City. That's how I met him. He had agreed to leave his artistic sanctuary in New York City to house himself temporarily in Kansas City for the play's World Premiere. That sounds pretty impressive, World Premiere, while in actuality, it just means that of all the places the playwright submits his play, the one theatre that does agree to mount the production makes a big deal out of the fact that this is the first time this particular play has been given a full-scale run. In theatre circles, they call this first production the play's World Premiere.

This is not to say the script was junk because the truth is that the play was fairly good, humane, funny, and we felt honored to have Mike. I say this as if I knew ahead of time that I would meet the playwright. I didn't. I was merely an actress who auditioned and got the part.

Our theatre was in a residential section of Midtown, and like many of the structures in Kansas City, it had once been a grand old residence that had been salvaged from the wrecking ball and now served as a lovely old grande dame theatre.

It wasn't too long after my audition that I received a phone call from Mike himself offering me the lead in his production. I was cast to play the young prostitute. The fact that I eagerly accepted the part says more about my thrill at being cast rather than about my thrill over the role. At the same time, in the acting business, one is always thankful to be working.

I showed up for the first read-through in a rather nervous frame of mind, which I believe is typical for anyone going into a new project. One has all those fears running around in the mind, such as, 'what if he hates me after he sees what I can (or cannot) bring to the role.' Or, 'what if I am one of those actresses who auditions better than she performs?' The usual self-doubting nonsense.

On this, our first night to meet as a complete cast, we were slated to have a first rehearsal, otherwise known in the business as a "read through." Script in hand, I opened the right side of one of the beautiful, tall doors to the theatre and stepped inside. The lobby was deserted and smelled slightly damp. Unsure where we were to meet, I looked first into the small sitting area off the main entrance, but no one was in there. So, script in hand, I pushed through the heavy black doors leading into the large theatre and found myself plunged into almost total darkness. I stood for a moment to acclimate my eyes to the stark change, and after my eyes adjusted to the light, I saw Mike sitting with the other actors down front near the stage. I walked up to them, and in an unaccustomed formality (for me) I extended my hand to Mike and we shook hands. I said something like, "Hi, I'm Kelly," to which he replied, "I know. I cast you in the lead."

Mike was a person who had frowned so much throughout his life that the edges of his mouth were permanently turned down. His hair was a dark brown and was so poker straight and precision layered that when he ran his fingers through his hair, as he did often, the hair sprang back every time into exactly the same position.

His eyes were large and green, both staring and vacant as if he might more easily find a far more interesting sight by gazing just above your head. He really didn't look into eyes very much, and I suppose one could say that Mike was good-looking if one could get past the obviously troubled expression that time had etched onto his face.

After all of the actors arrived for this, our first get-together, Mike began the meeting by introducing himself and offering other general details about his life. Although he seemed more animated when talking strictly about the play, he did volunteer, "I am not completely unfamiliar with Kansas City. I have an Aunt who lives here, and I've had relatives living here my entire life. We are an old Kansas City family."

That first night, his manner depressed me slightly, and furthermore, he seemed emotionally disturbed and kept folding and unfolding the corner of his script the entire time he talked. Then, after his introduction, he invited each of us to stand and tell a little bit about ourselves, and once that was done, he clapped his hands together and announced, "Okay, let's get started."

Despite the fact that my first impression of Mike was somewhat unfavorable, we did progress as friends (although I find this is pretty inevitable when you are working closely with another person on a project). Even so, he seemed to have singled me out as a confidante, and we often had lunch together before we began rehearsals each day. On one such occasion, he attempted to explain events that led up to his having written this fairly successful play.

"My Uncle died," he said, "and since he had no children, he left me a comfortable amount of money, and I believe that was the beginning of my problems because I immediately quit work to devote my total days to writing. Looking back on the experience, I can see clearly how unprepared I was - or anyone is, for that matter - for life-changing events, whether they represent gains or losses. All change, whether it be winning, losing, marrying, divorcing, losing a loved one to death - all change represents stress."

I really didn't know what to say, so I said, "Okay," as if to indicate that I was following him (which I wasn't). But whatever it was that he was trying to express seemed to weigh heavily on his mind as he continued, "I suppose my attempted escape at that low point was the birth of this play." And then he asked me, "Did you know that having a place to escape to each day can actually be a healthy diversion?"

He seemed anxious to make a point while at the same time seemed anxious to get my input. He obviously needed validation of some sort, yet I didn't know how to tell him that, although I could tell something deep was bothering him, I didn't know what the heck he was driving at. I wanted to say, 'Mike, just come out with it. Speak in more simple language, please.'

But he often continued voicing his elusive topics. "God, I hate daylight," he once said suddenly. "In the light of day, everything is supposed to make sense. Bankers balance books. Wall Street rises or it falls. Business America drives through the cleaners and picks up their clean shirts. People eat donuts and cereal for breakfast. Daylight is for authentic people who have somewhere to go and something to contribute. It isn't for night creeps like me who are living off some old dead man's money."

I could hear the guilt underlying his words, and although I wanted to point out, some old dead man! Mike, that is your uncle you are talking about. I instead said something like, "Mike, if you feel that bad, why don't you just get a job and quit writing. Sounds to me as if you don't really like writing."

Upon hearing my comment, he looked at me as if I had committed some stupid chess move and said, "Jobs are a waste of time. They hog the best moments of one's life, and they are a big fat excuse to stop thinking. Working is the sane man's form of basket weaving. He kills time for the next 50 years of his life so he won't have to worry about what to do with his excess time."

These tirades sometimes seemed to relieve pressure, yet he would continue, "I need someone to help me bridge that gap between where I am and where I should be. Am I wrong to think these things? Does no one else concern himself with such mania? Are the majority voices simply silent? That is what I am most afraid of. I'm afraid there are others who feel as I do, yet who do nothing about it. Furthermore, I fear that most of us have given up, and are busy slipping into other things, into drugs or into doubts, ultimately into oblivion. I fear that, in its defeated state, mankind is simply letting the sheer popularity of the documented formula be the accepted and unquestioned formula for all."

"Documented formula?" I asked. Then I quickly decided that Mike was possibly insane, and if I had any sense, I should probably get far, far away from him.

The waitress brought us our check, but when I tried to stand, it became apparent that during all of this time spent listening to a half-crazy man express himself, I had drunk more wine than I thought. When he saw me sway, he put a protective arm around me, and in this manner we departed the restaurant.

On the day of opening night, Mike called me to indicate that he wanted us to drive together to the theatre. I said that sounded like a fun idea, so he extended an invitation to me to come and spend the rest of the afternoon with him at his Aunt's house. It was around 3:00 p.m. already, and although we didn't need to be at the theatre until 7:00 p.m., he thought it might be a good idea if he came now and picked me up. Somewhat reluctantly, I agreed.

He picked me up and we rode back in his aunt's perfectly preserved Oldsmobile. I leaned over, read the ridiculously low odometer on the car, and said, "When was the last time anyone drove this car?"

Rare for him, Mike laughed, "My aunt doesn't drive anymore. Even when she did drive, she never went any further than to the grocery store and back."

"Mike," I said, "do you realize how many people would love to get their hands on an old, well-preserved creampuff like this?"

He nodded, but then he immediately frowned and began to watch the road as if there might be roadblocks ahead. He was obviously uncomfortable while driving.

There was something about his aunt's house that took my breath away. It wasn't so much its beauty that left me speechless, because to be honest, it was in a somewhat rundown condition. It wasn't falling down, mind you, although there was chipped paint here and there. Also, the shrubs had been neglected, and a window shutter or two could have been straightened, but all three stories of the house stood like a proud old lady. It towered, an aged and beautiful ball queen, once stately and proper, now mature and slightly bowed.
Mike pulled around to the back of the house into a driveway and switched off the ignition. I sat gazing at the house and said, "Man, they surely don't build houses like this anymore." Mike shrugged and said, "My grandfather was an architect. He designed and built the house for my aunt and uncle as a wedding present."

From the car window, I could see a deck flush with the second level, built up from the ground on stakes. Vines grew on one side of the house, but in other places, leaves had died, and the effect gave the house a brownish, dirty wash that still could not hide its majesty.

"It is really too big for my aunt now that she is alone," Mike said, "but it's her home. This is the only place she has ever lived."

We got out of the car and walked around to the front of the house. I tried looking straight up as we walked, but kept stumbling over rocks in the driveway.

"Sorry," he said, "but I only have the front door key with me. This place has a million keys."

I could see how that would be possible because, in addition to a front door, the house had a second floor with doors as well as a back door, two side doors, and another outside door leading to someplace else.

While standing on the porch waiting for Mike to unlock the door, I looked straight up, where I could see that the third story virtually disappeared into the trees. From what I could see of the house through the trees, it appeared to give the impression that the house had some type of wings - not wings of flight, but mythical wings. I noticed that it also had gargoyles, dormer windows, and a judas window.

Our noise on the front porch triggered from inside the nervous yipping of what sounded like a small dog. Mike, jiggling the keys, searching for the key to the front door, finally found and unlocked the massive front door, which, creaking fully back, opened onto an enclosed porch that was completely furnished with thickly cushioned blonde rattan furniture upholstered in large black and purple flowers. And, though it seemed odd, once inside the house, I could no longer hear the barking dog.

There was a brown grand piano that sat in a small niche in the living room, the lid down and the keyboard covered tightly.

"Mike," I asked, "do you play the piano?"

"Sometimes I do," he said, "I sit and play here some nights, yes."

I had a strange urge to march over to the piano, and in a grand romantic gesture, raise the keyboard cover, sit down, and play a haunting Chopin nocturne. I could actually play Chopin's Etude Op. 10, No. 3, but it was extremely difficult being written in four sharps, and there was no way I had the piece committed to memory.

"I can play the piano too," I said, "But I need music. I'm not one who can sit down and play by ear."

Mike looked at me with the slightest frown. He seemed troubled or tired, and he ran his fingers through his hair a couple of times. "There is nothing wrong with that," he said.
He walked over to the piano, sat down, and raised the keyboard cover as if to play. He stared at the keyboard for a moment, then reached his right hand and rested it lightly on the keys before he played a few notes. Then he played ripples, then soft chords. A small rhythm established, he brought his left hand to the keyboard and employed a floating accompaniment which built until he sat enthralled in the charming sounds he was creating, while with his head slightly bowed, eyes closed, he played, seemingly unaware of anything surrounding him except this lovely and mournful melody.

I had seated myself on a nearby, ancient-looking love seat, which served to allow me a grander view of the house. I looked beyond the niche as far as I could see, looking up at tall, almost 12-foot ceilings. This was the style of house where, in old movies, lots of people found themselves congregated on rainy nights, whose daytime hours had been spent sleeping until tea time, and who, in the evenings, sat down to long dinner tables with candlesticks. Guests would arrive, beautifully dressed, and they would eat for the entire duration of the movie. After dinner, Sherry would be poured from sparkling crystal decanters. Then the guests would adjourn to a drawing room and cluster around a crackling fire for men to smoke cigars and women to play the piano, while invariably, someone upstairs was being murdered.

"Mike," I said, "this house is positively magnificent!"

"Thank you," he said, as he continued to play. Did he like the house? Really? Was he pleased to be in my company? I could never tell - couldn't read him at all.

I continued, "You never told me you were surrounded by such poetry."
He stopped playing, shut the keyboard cover, and stood, "Let me give you a complete tour of the house."

When he took my hand, his hand felt warm. It wasn't cold like the rest of him, and I found this surprising. His hands also felt soft and without calluses, hands that obviously did only sensitive types of work.

We walked through an arch into an adjoining formal dining room, which contained wood-carved, French-looking antiques.

The dining table with eight chairs occupied center stage, and against one wall stood a china cabinet full of tarnished silver pieces sitting, for all their unpolished splendor, behind a locked glass door.

Mike saw me looking at the silver, and he said, "Now, you're not going to come back here and rip the place off, are you?"

Maybe that was his idea of a joke, but it hurt my feelings, and my immediate instinct was to say, 'I think you had better take me home.' But we still had a play to do tonight. I had to hold it together. We wound our way down a long hallway and ended up at the base of a curving staircase. There was a serious lack of lighting in the hallway, and my eyes needed time to adjust before I could climb the staircase. In the dim, I could barely make out the wooden staircase, carpeted only in the center of the stair rungs with dark oriental carpet. Cautiously, I held onto the curving railing and made the climb.

As we neared the top of the stairs, I spied a man in a collarless suit peering at me from his prominent position at the top of the stairs in the form of a large oil portrait that hung on the wall.

"That is my uncle, now deceased," Mike said.

Once here on the second level of the house, I could see that the staircase continued to curve up one more floor, but we turned left and walked past two closed doors all the way to a door at the end of the hall. The one window at the top of this second floor was draped with heavy emerald green velvet draperies, and because the setting sun was almost totally blocked out by this heaviness, I found the hallway especially dark and dreary.

Very softly, Mike knocked twice at the door at the end of the hall, then we entered. At first, I was overcome by the pungent smell of roses. The room smelled like a sickeningly sweet, artificial rose garden, and directly in front of us sat a very elderly lady sitting in a comfortable-looking, fluffy chair. She wore a pink robe, and it was literally speckled with cigarette burns.

Mike stepped up to the lady, bent down, and shouted loudly in her ear, "Aunt Vi, I would like for you to meet my leading actress, Kelly."

Aunt Vi sat, cigarette burning in one hand, iced-down drink in the other.

"How do you do?" she set the drink down and extended a frail hand, palm down, as if I were an old gentleman caller who would likely kiss her hand.

I took her hand, awkwardly, "Very pleased to meet you," I said.

Mike gestured toward a nearby rocker where he waved, intending for me to sit, so I sat. Then, he crossed the room and positioned himself on the hammock in front of his aunt's chair.

"So," he shouted to Aunt Vi, "what have you been doing today?"

"Oh, just busy, busy business," she smiled and almost giggled as she took a sip of her iced-down amber colored liquid. Then, she dabbed with a lace handkerchief at her watery left eye.

"Mrs. Brown keeping you busy?" he asked in a gentle tone of voice that I had never heard before.

This last comment was obviously a private joke between Mike and his elderly aunt, because as they talked, Mrs. Brown, a robust and smiling black woman dressed in a nurse's uniform, entered the room. I sat watching the ease with which the three of them visited with one another. Mike seemed much more comfortable with these rather remote characters than I had ever seen him with anyone else. It's no wonder that he acts so odd at times, I thought. He lives a unique lifestyle suspended in time, a place situated somewhere between the impersonal modern-day zoo of New York City and this formal convention of the proper past. Yet, here in his aunt's house, he is surrounded by a combination of heavy nostalgia, moldy vacant rooms, and stately excess: an oppression that often hangs over the once regal, grown old.

Soon, Mike rose to excuse himself from the rest of us and announced, "I'm going to shower and clean up. You three visit." He gestured towards me, "I'll be back for you," he said, "as soon as I am cleaned up. Then we'll leave for the theatre." With that, he left the room.

His aunt was charming, yet I found her difficult to talk to. She was in a delightfully childish world all her own. Further, I observed that Mrs. Brown spoke to her as if she were her little pet poodle. Soon, Mrs. Brown began to direct her conversation toward me.

"I heard lot o' nice things 'bout you," she said.

That surprised me. Mike gave no indication that he thought about anything except his unnamed misery. He was more often than not strange and quiet.

"Really?" I tried to pass off my surprise as modesty, yet I became curious.

"Yes," she said simply. Then she looked out the short window to the left of the bedroom fireplace and directed the rest of her comments outside.

These two were suitable company for each other, however. Aunt Vi had her cigarettes, her mixed cocktail, her memories, while Mrs. Brown seemed to be the keeper and foreman of the house. Aunt Vi had built-in companionship, and Mrs. Brown was able to move easily in a world of dignity, albeit in the big house with its archaic air. Both women owned different sides of a type of comfortable fantasy.

"Mike, he sit up late at night and writes," Mrs. Brown said, "sometimes he sleep all day. He write late into the night, sometimes."

Aunt Vi seemed to listen attentively, an enigmatic smile gracing her expression, the grimace of innocence unmistakable on her face. For all she knew, we could have been discussing geraniums. Her cigarette burned dangerously long, and I watched an ash fall into her lap. Mrs. Brown jumped up with a tissue and an ashtray.

"Auntie," she said in her best scolding voice, "you gone burn down yo' house someday. You know that? Gone burn it plum down!"

Aunt Vi smiled and said, "Busy, busy, business."

The little dog I had heard earlier ran into the room, ran up to the foot of my chair, and began to sniff at me, poking his cold nose into my ankles. I bent to pet it, but as I did, I realized

I felt short of breath and needed fresh air because the rose fragrance had begun to stifle me quite a bit.

As I stood, I addressed Mrs. Brown, "Where is your bathroom, please?"

Mrs. Brown jumped up very hospitably, walked quickly to the door, and pointed, "down the hall, this side."

I walked out of the room into the hall, shut the bedroom door, and took a deep breath of stale, though fragrance-free air. Standing there, my hand still on the doorknob, I felt renewed surprise to find the hallway so oppressively dark. It would seem appropriate to tiptoe, since my initial urge was to snoop, so I crept as silently as possible down the hall and walked right up to the portrait hanging on the wall.

The man in the portrait resembled a middle-aged Mike. He had the same straight brown hair, same high cheekbones and steely green eyes, had the strong, prominent jaw, but there wasn't the deep furrow that Mike carried across his brow. This man looked considerably happier than Mike ever did. After surveying the portrait in depth, I began to descend the stairs, but at the bottom of the stairs, I found myself in somewhat of a maze, because I hadn't really paid much attention to how we had come up the stairs. To my right stood a door, slightly ajar, so I walked to it and cautiously peeked inside. I could feel moisture in the air, could see that the mirror above the sink was slightly steamed over, and I realized that I had happened upon the same bathroom in which Mike had just taken a shower and had now left. So, I went in and closed the door.

Fat pink ceramic tiles covered the floor and went all the way up to the ceiling. The bathtub fixtures, also pink, looked completely original. The bathtub had big claw feet, and the sink was a thick, marbled pedestal piece. There was a multi-colored, braided rug that lay next to the tub, and it was damp. I saw that Mike's tennis shoes were sitting under the sink pedestal. His razor, also damp, lay on top of the sink.

I moved to open the door of the medicine chest to continue my clandestine inspection, but decided instead to subtly announce my presence, so I flushed the commode. When water came swirling back into the bowl, I opened the bathroom door, stepped into the dark hall, and walked directly into Mike.

"I thought I heard you come down," he said. "Come into the kitchen with me. I still have to wash my hair, and I am going to have to do it in the kitchen sink. The water pressure is so low in the bathtub that I feel like my hair gets rinsed better in the sink."

He stepped briefly into the bathroom, opened the medicine chest, and retrieved a bottle of shampoo. Then, he took my hand and led me to the end of the darkness, where we turned a corner and entered the kitchen.

The kitchen was the biggest disappointment in the house. It was cozy, more cozy than any other room so far, but it was small and common. I couldn't understand how any four-course meals could be drummed up in a kitchen this dysfunctional. There was a simple table with two chairs sitting under the window. A large free-standing range and refrigerator stood side by side, and along the other free wall stood cabinets and a sink. The countertops were covered with fat white ceramic tiles with little blue lines. That was it!

I seated myself in one of the kitchen chairs, the one facing the sink, and I watched Mike bend over and wet his hair.

"Hey, Mike," I began, silly, nervous chatter, "this kitchen reminds me of one I once saw while visiting France," I said.

He looked up for a moment, angling to keep the running water out of his eyes.

I continued, "But France was beautiful in its old-charm way. I mean, things were old but still functional." I noticed that he was still looking at me. Was he listening? Or, was he dissecting the sentence?

I continued my random prattle, "Did you know that in France, they don't have potato chips in bags? They make them fresh every day, from real potatoes, like they do their bread. Fresh every day. You can find these fresh potato chips in all the bars…"

Mike lunged forward a little, still hanging his wet head squarely into the sink and laughed, "My god, you sound like something out of a John Fowles novel."

"What do you mean?" I asked.

"You sound lost. Suspended in a dream state," he placed syllabic emphasis on the last two words.

I felt a bit insulted because he had made the statement with ever so slightly a bit of mocking harshness. "I never know what you are going to say," he continued.

He was now studying me through a wink, with one eye closed.

"I can't keep up with your mind." He had a way of harshly punctuating the last word in his sentences, "Can't quite figure it out."

So that was it. He has been busy trying to figure me out. This odd confession, the equivalence of mental voyeurism, unsettled me, so I stood with the intention of heading back upstairs to the safety of Aunt Vi and Mrs. Brown.

Mike grabbed the towel to quickly dry off the dripping water from his head, "Do you know why I like you?" he asked.

Standing perfectly still and somewhat miffed, I said, "I didn't know you did like me."

"Well, I do," he said.

"I think you might be imagining things about me that aren't there," I said.

He continued, "Maybe I'm just jealous. Maybe I'm envious that you are emotional, that you possess the simplicity to be happy."

"Simplicity? Did you just insult me?" I asked.

"Easily amused, you are," he continued. "With all that you have and all that you lack, at least you aren't miserable."

I looked at him, stunned, as I had not, to this point, known misery to be a part of our conversation. But, before I could form an opinion about the tone of our conversation, he reacted quickly by straightening his stance, towel thrown aside, he brought both hands together for emphasis and said, "I'm miserable!"

I was at a loss as to what to say or how to react to this. I didn't know if I should try to console or just listen. I didn't know if I should voice an opinion or merely offer pure silence as a cushion, didn't know whether to mirror him, to deny him, or whether to simply ignore him. As if this type of sudden revelation hadn't found me unsettled enough, as if to top off his surprising outburst, he walked toward me, put his arms around me, and kissed me on the mouth.

I rather sank back onto the chair.

"You don't like people looking at you, do you?" he admonished.

I looked at him, stunned, "Why is it that I am suddenly under the microscope?"

"I didn't realize it was sudden," he smiled. "I've observed you for some time now. I find it quite curious how actors can parade overtly in front of hundreds of strangers, but they are truly naked without their props."

Mike both frightened and excited me, and judging from the sneer-like expression on his face, it became obvious that he was insulting me and was becoming aroused at the same time. I was afraid to look at him, and I was afraid to look away. Stepping to the side of my chair now, he began a slight rubbing massage at the back of my neck. I glanced at him and saw an amused curl on his lips, one side of his mouth curving down as he seemed to be fighting the urge to smile. Then he kissed me again. This was a premeditated fever, and I caught it. It had been passed on to me now. This was clearly passion and nothing else. Raw passion.

After that afternoon, Mike and I became an unusual item. He was sometimes tender and sometimes cruel. He would speak words of affection one day, then completely withdraw into stony silence the next. He would often make plans, then seem to forget all about them - never mention them again. I didn't feel as if I knew him, not ever. If it was his intention to keep me guessing, he did a very good job.

It is human nature for a lover to want to feel safe in a relationship, and I believe that the absence of safety in our relationship was the very quality that made me tense and unhappy the more time I spent around him. It was as if his darkness was beginning to become my darkness. He was absorbing me.

One day, when we were in his room, I noticed something I had not seen before: a large, steel suitcase. It was obviously old, an antique probably, and I commented on it.

"What's in the big suitcase?" I asked.
"You've never seen this suitcase," he said, looking down at some papers he was sorting, "because it's usually in the closet."

He volunteered no further information, and I knew better than to pry, so I let the conversation drop.

"I'm going through some things," he said as he flipped over one paper and proceeded to study the next one. "Actually, I'm packing to leave," he said.

"To leave?!" I was incredulous.

He looked up at me with a steady gaze, "Did you think I would stay in this one-horse town indefinitely?"

I was incapable of voicing my shock. I knew he was cold and mostly uncommunicative, but I had no idea that he would just one day leave without any discussion whatsoever. Or, maybe this was the discussion. Maybe this was all I got - an accidental stumbling upon the facts.

"Had you planned to discuss this with me?" I asked.

"Discuss what, my leaving?" He put down the paper in his hand, and his countenance was completely without expression except for that perpetual frown.

I became so angry at myself that I developed a hot flush throughout my body. I folded my hands together and touched my nose as if to force my mouth to stay shut. Truly, what had I expected? He had been right all along; I did live in a dream state. I did shut my eyes to reality. I chose to believe what I wanted to believe despite evidence to the contrary. He had never, not really, ever given me any reason to think that I mattered to him in any way except to serve as his leading lady in the play, then later to serve as his lover in bed. I was the one who had filled in the spaces.

I walked over to the old trunk and lifted the lid.

"What are you doing?" he lunged, now angry.

Inside the trunk were several pictures of different women. I snatched up one. Acting like a spoiled child, I held up the picture and shouted, "Who is this?"

"S-h-h-h," he said as he gently walked toward me, "Aunt Vi will hear us."

I snatched up another picture, "Who's this?"

He caught my arm, "Kelly," he said, "why are you getting upset? Don't you realize this is just your ego reacting?"

I couldn't believe his calm. He was acting as if I were the crazy one. He treated me like he was the nurse and I was the psychiatric patient. Suddenly, it became clear. He hadn't planned any explanations whatsoever. Perhaps none were needed. Perhaps it was an okay thing to do to just leave town and never tell the woman you have been screwing that you are leaving. She can just call up Aunt Vi's house one fine day, ask for Mike, and Mrs. Brown can say, 'I'm sorry. He done took the plane back to New York.' And, she can sit there like a fool with the phone in her hand, hot tears behind her eyes, and on the other end of the line, and Mrs. Brown can be saying, 'You there, missus? You there?'

I stood and began to gather my things. Mike looked at me, now puzzled. I would do the same to him. I would walk out without giving him any indication that I was leaving.

I walked out of the door of his attic room. By this time, I knew the house well enough that I could show myself out. But he followed me. He took my arm. He said, "Kelly."

But I said nothing. If I were indeed something out of a John Fowles novel, as he once said, then I would act like something out of a John Fowles novel. I would walk away like Allison did in The Magus. I would walk without looking back, and I would walk without saying a word, because were I to speak, which I didn't, I would have said: A wave washed me into your life, Mike, but a choice walks me away. I shall walk away from you as far as the east is from the west, and should you follow me, we shall merely form a perpetual circle. I don't remember getting into my car, and I don't remember the drive home. I only remember that as I turned off the gravel driveway from his Aunt Vi's house, I looked up at the trees that hugged the third story of the house and noticed that they had begun to turn beautiful colors of gold, red, and brown. Perhaps they had been turning those colors for some time now, but I had just begun to notice.

www.ingramcontent.com/pod-product-compliance
Lightning Source LLC
Chambersburg PA
CBHW070954120726
47910CB00004B/1236